NICK

Texas Rascals Book Three

LORI WILDE

"I am not working with him. It's out of the question." Michele Mallory, Texas State Trooper, crossed her arms and glared at the arrogant, lean-muscled male slouching on one corner of her superior officer's desk.

Why did this man have to be devastatingly handsome with that thatch of coal-black hair and those mesmerizing brown eyes? Good-looking he might be, but Michele thought "Nick" Nickerson was also the most infuriating individual she'd ever met.

"Me?" Feigning innocence, Nickerson arched his eyebrows. "What'd I ever do to you?"

"Now, Michele," Lieutenant Ray Charboneau began, but she cut him off.

"Don't patronize me, Lieutenant. I'm dead serious. The last time I worked with this joker..." She jerked a thumb at Nickerson. "He almost got me killed."

Nick shook his head as if Michele were a wayward child conjuring up an unbelievable tale. "Exaggerating a bit, aren't you, Mish?"

If looks were darts, Nickerson would have been a sieve.

"It's Officer Mallory. And I don't consider taking a bullet an exaggeration."

Nick clicked his tongue. "Who disobeyed my command and went running off after the perp alone?"

"Disobeyed you? You weren't my commanding officer. We were partners."

"I was the senior trooper on the scene."

"Kiss my backside, Nickerson."

"Be glad to. You name the time and place. I'll be there, puckered up and ready to go." Nickerson smirked.

Michele's fingers itched to slap his smug face. "In your dreams."

"That's a lot of animosity for such an attractive girl."

"I am not a girl. I'm twenty-seven years old and more woman than you could ever manage."

"Yes, ma'am." The sassy gleam in Nickerson's eyes was purely wicked. He'd been baiting her. "You sure are."

Michele gulped, remembering that fateful night last December. The night she'd lain bleeding in the truck stop parking lot along Interstate 35. The night Nickerson had kissed her. A night she regretted but somehow couldn't stop thinking about.

"Excuse me, but could you two put your personal differences aside while we review this case?" Lieutenant Charboneau spread his palms, indicating the manila folder on his desk.

"But that's my point, Lieutenant." Michele paced the small office, her hands moving to punctuate her words. "I can't work with him. He's undisciplined, arrogant, a real loose cannon. I pride my reputation too much to be harnessed with him. I even lodged an official complaint against him after the Harbarger incident, but no one took me seriously, and I resent that."

"Internal Affairs exonerated Nick." Lieutenant Ray Charboneau ran a hand through his thinning hair. "Michele, I realize Nickerson sometimes uses an unorthodox approach to criminal investigation, but you can't deny he's one of our finest undercover officers. No one can argue his arrest and conviction record."

Michele gritted her teeth. She smelled defeat. The last thing she wanted in the whole wide world was to be paired with Nickerson again.

"So why send me on the case? If he's so great, why not let Mr. Wonderful go alone?"

"Have a seat, Michele," Lieutenant Charboneau said.

Agitated, Michele perched on the edge of a stiff-backed chair in front of the lieutenant's desk. Chin in the air, she avoided eye contact with Nickerson.

The three weeks they'd spent together on the Harbarger investigation last December were forever etched in her brain. Three weeks tracking the truckers moving stolen merchandise from El Paso to Amarillo. Three weeks drinking rot-gut coffee from paper cups and eating fast-food hamburgers from greasy sacks. Three weeks cooped up in a patrol car with Nickerson.

Not exactly her idea of heaven, but if the truth be told, it had been the most exciting time of her life, despite the fact she'd come out of the escapade with a bullet in her arm and a healthy dislike for the cocky Mr. Nickerson and his questionable police tactics.

"This is an unusual case," Lieutenant Charboneau continued. "Involving the Racing Commission."

"Ah," Nick said, interest flickering in his dark eyes. "Politics."

Michele dropped her gaze, hoping Nick hadn't noticed that she'd been staring. As much as she wanted to deny it, the man fascinated her. Something about the way he moved, so self-confident and assured, demanded her attention. Maybe that was why he irritated her. She did not wish to be intrigued by a modern-day Wyatt Earp.

"Yeah," Charboneau said grimly. "This is coming down from the governor's office. You were handpicked for the assignment, Nickerson." The lieutenant paused.

"Go on," Nick prompted.

Charboneau's eyes met Michele's. "That's where you come in, Mallory. We need someone who knows horses."

True enough. As the only child of a judge with a yen for horses and a blue-blooded mother who was a retired jockey turned riding teacher, Michele had been able to ride before she could walk. To escape the turmoil of family strife, she'd often fled on horseback, flying free and unfettered across the dry, West Texas prairie.

"I need you two to go undercover," Lieutenant Charboneau said. "Together."

Nick leaned forward and rubbed his hands along his blue-jean-clad legs. "Tell me more, Lieutenant. You're singing my song."

Michele peeked at Nick. A shelf of ebony hair spilled down the collar of his leather jacket. The thin, straight scar riding his jawbone gleamed silver in the fluorescent lighting.

She knew he coveted a position with the Texas Rangers. Since the Harbarger bust, Nick had been promoted to sergeant, and he was always on the lookout for special assignments. This one had been dropped neatly into his lap by the governor himself.

Too bad she didn't share Nick's enthusiasm for covert operations. Michele preferred uniform duty, hated the deception inherent in undercover work. She was a lousy liar and an even worse sneak, two areas where Nickerson excelled.

Ray Charboneau toyed with a rubber band. "The Racing Commission believes there is a new synthetic drug, undetectable by blood or urine analysis, that they suspect is being administered to racehorses."

"What?" Michele got to her feet, boots smacking against the linoleum.

Scientific technology had honed drug testing to a degree so precise, they could detect chemicals in even the most minute doses. She knew that if a trainer who used cocaine simply touched his horse's muzzle, the animal would test positive for the drug. Michele had assumed the sophisticated advances in detection would make racehorse doping obsolete. Apparently, she had underestimated the ingenuity of the criminal mind.

"There have been a few incidents in recent weeks concerning horses boarded at the Triple Fork Stables outside of Rascal, Texas." Charboneau paused. "Some of the horses were expected to finish dead last in their respective races and instead came out of nowhere to topple the favorites."

Michele had heard about that.

"As you may know," her supervisor continued. "The governor owns a championship-caliber Thoroughbred who's been coming up short against these turbocharged winners. He isn't pleased."

"And despite repeated testing, these horses keep coming up clean," Nick guessed. Leaning forward, he rested his elbows on his knees and steepled his fingers.

"Exactly."

"Where do we come in?" Michele asked.

"I've arranged jobs for you at the Triple Fork." Lieutenant Charboneau leaned back in his chair and folded his hands over his ample belly. "Everyone is under suspicion. Trainers, vets, stable hands, jockeys. Anyone who comes in contact with the horses."

"Any common threads?" Nick's expression darkened. Michele could almost hear his mental cogs whirling.

Charboneau shook his head. "No. All seventeen of the suspect horses had different owners, trainers, and different jockeys. The only common denominator is the Triple Fork. That's why I've set you up there."

Nick nodded.

"You've got to be very careful," the lieutenant continued. "We don't know how widespread this doping is. Might be local. Might include organized crime. Might even be a political backlash against the governor and the Racing Commission. Right now, we don't have much to go on."

"Any other states experiencing similar problems?" Nick asked.

"None that we know of."

"You believe the drug is being manufactured in Texas?" Michele tucked an errant strand of hair behind her ear.

"We suspect that, yes." Charboneau nodded.

"So what's the plan?" Nick sent Michele a sidelong gaze.

"We have another team watching Mario Martuchi, the local mobster we believe is connected to the racing business. But basically, you and Mallory will be on your own. You'll be living at the ranch, and we'll set up a meeting place in the nearby town of Marfa for weekly reports."

"I still don't see why you need me," Michele interrupted.

She had to admit this case captured her curiosity. She would love being around horses. But the thought of working with Nickerson again made her want to break out in hives.

"We need a team, Mallory."

"What about Jeff Travis? He used to be a horse trainer. Why can't he go undercover with Captain Courageous here?" She jerked her head in Nickerson's direction.

"Ah, well," Charboneau hedged. "That's a little complicated."

"How complicated?"

"For one thing, Travis is knee-deep in another case."

"And?" Michele stared at her boss.

"Travis is actually from Marfa. Yeah, small world. So he can't go undercover in Rascal in case someone local recognizes him."

"Okay, why not someone else?"

"This is a special case." Charboneau took a sip from the coffee cup on his desk and pulled a face that told her the coffee must have gone cold.

The hairs on the back of her neck prickled a warning. There was something awfully fishy about this setup. She didn't like it. Not one bit.

Charboneau shifted in his seat, pushed the coffee cup away from him, and let out his breath in a long, slow sigh. "The Triple Fork was looking for a husband-and-wife team to serve as ranch manager and cook, and the opportunity was too good to pass up." Ducking his head, he dropped his gaze, suddenly fascinated by the rubber band in his hands.

Michele blinked. Evidently, she hadn't heard Charboneau correctly. Forcing a smile, she cleared her throat. "Excuse me, Lieutenant, but I must have misunderstood. I thought I just heard you say you hired Nickerson and me out as a husband-and-wife team."

Charboneau winced. "Hmm. Well, I did."

Michele bit down on her tongue and counted to ten. "I don't believe this. You made these arrangements without telling me?"

"I'm telling you now, Mallory."

"No way. Not doing it. I definitely will not pretend to be married to this...this...person." Michele waved a hand at Nick. The mere idea of it sent heat waves skipping down her nerve endings. Pretend to be Nick Nickerson's wife? Not bloody likely!

Nick unfurled his lean, hard body from the corner of Charboneau's desk, drew himself up to his full six foot, two inches, and squared off with Michele toe-to-toe. He stared down at her with the intensity of a hawk on the hunt.

A shiver ran through her, as cold and unexpected as if someone had dumped ice cubes down her collar.

Nickerson's eyes glittered.

Michele gulped.

She had convinced herself the feelings he'd stirred in her during the three weeks they'd spent on stakeout were nothing but a weird aberration. Yet if that were true, why was she suddenly longing to have his firm lips pressed hard against her own? Why did she ache to feel his fingers slide deliciously through her hair?

"I won't do it," she said.

"Why is that? Don't think you can handle the pressure of being my wife?" Nickerson cocked his head.

"I don't think a diamondback rattlesnake could handle being your wife." Michele tossed her head along with the retort.

A sardonic smile crossed Nickerson's face. "I see you haven't lost that sharp-edged tongue of yours."

"And it's clear you're as arrogant as ever."

"We don't have to like each other to work together." Nick arched an eyebrow. "I'm a professional. It wouldn't bother me one whit to pretend to play house with you, Mallory."

"I'm as professional as you are, Nickerson. More so. I follow correct police procedure. I don't recklessly endanger fellow troopers."

"That's low, Mallory, even for you." His chin was set firm and hard, his face just inches from hers.

"Oh, yeah?" Michele thrust out her chest, drew herself up to her full five foot, nine inches, and kept her gaze locked on his. She refused to look away, to let him win.

"Yeah."

Restrained anger flashed in Nick's black eyes, and

Michele's heart lurched wildly. Strangely enough, she found his controlled hostility exciting.

Charboneau pushed up from his chair. He went around the desk to step between them. "Are you kids finished taunting each other? We've got a job to do."

"Mallory instigated the whole thing."

"What? You're trying to pin this argument on me?" Michele's face flushed hotly. She jammed her hands on her hips and glared at Nick.

"Hey, you're the one refusing to work with me, not the other way around, Goldilocks."

Michele gritted her teeth. "You're a fine one for assigning blame. Who left me at that truck stop by myself?"

"You weren't supposed to go after Harbarger alone," he replied quietly.

His grimace told Michele that her comment had struck to the bone. Immediately contrite, she bit down on her tongue. It hadn't been Nick's fault that a fugitive's bullet had torn a chunk from her arm. He'd told her not to leave the squad car and to call for backup if trouble arose. But determined to prove she was tough enough to handle things on her own, Michele had stubbornly defied him.

She wanted to take back those words, but it was too late. She could apologize, of course, but then Nickerson might think her weak. Lifting her chin, she tossed her head.

"You two are exactly alike." Charboneau snorted. "Hard-headed as hell and more conceited than Satan himself."

"We are not!" they said in unison.

Charboneau shook his head. "There you go, proving my point. Both of you always have to be in control. No wonder neither of you is married. Who could put up with you?"

Michele slanted Nickerson a sidelong glance. Perhaps there was a grain of truth to the lieutenant's words. She liked having things her way, and so did Nick.

"Sit back down, both of you," Charboneau demanded. "And let's go over the details one by one."

Like two wary jungle cats, they circled each other before settling down in their respective chairs. Michele's pulse dashed at a sprinter's pace. Taking a deep breath, she folded her hands in her lap.

Nick Nickerson was the most opinionated, overbearing, egotistical jerk she'd ever had the misfortune to meet, and now she was going to be stuck posing as his new bride!

2

The idea of working with Michele Mallory again had Nick's libido pumping into overdrive. What was it about the woman that so aroused him?

Sure she was cute, with that fiery golden hair confined in a sleek French braid. He suppressed an urge to lean over, pluck the hairpins from her controlled coiffure, and let the golden flames tumble down her slender shoulders.

Who could ignore those luscious lips, that delicate nose, and her oh-so-fine backside encased enticingly in the stretchy material of her trooper's uniform? And that heady scent of hers, pure cinnamon—hot, spicy, and refreshingly different.

Nick had his pick of attractive women, so why did he find Mallory so darned appealing? He admired the way she stood up to him. Michele Mallory stuck to her principles no matter what the price, and his own miserable childhood had taught him to respect that. The strong survived. The weak remained victims their entire lives, and Michele was anything but a victim.

Neither was he.

Unpleasant, twenty-year-old memories tumbled through

his head. And as clear as yesterday, his mind replayed the memory of his drunken, snarling father slamming his fist into his mother's face.

For months, Nick had secretly been working out in the high school gym, preparing for just such a confrontation. Although his knees had knocked in fear, Nick managed to step between his parents, grab his father's wrist, and order him out of the house. Amazingly enough, the old man had left for good.

Even now, remembering the heady power he had felt while protecting his mother, a thrill of victory ran through Nick.

Yes, Michele Mallory reminded him a lot of himself, and he wondered about her background. Had her early life been as turbulent as his own?

What did it matter? She wasn't his type. Not at all. He preferred gentle females who readily acquiesced, not head-strong tomboys who disobeyed orders and got themselves shot. He grunted under his breath as another memory flashed through his mind.

From the minute they'd been assigned together, Nick had fought an overwhelming attraction to Michele. He had kept his mouth shut for three weeks, trying to maintain his professional distance and never letting on how he felt about her.

And then all hell had broken loose.

In vivid detail, Nick remembered that fateful night seven months ago when he'd returned to that truck stop parking lot to find that Michele had abandoned the cruiser in solo pursuit of their quarry.

Recollecting the event brought the bitter taste of fear into his mouth again. Etched in his mind was the sight of flashing lights spilling red and blue circles into the night.

The patrol car door had stood open. The radio crackled

with warped voices. He'd scanned the area, searching desperately for any sign of Michele.

With his gun drawn, Nick had run through the massive parking lot, ducking behind eighteen wheelers, dodging vans and pickup trucks, his heart racing.

The sound of diesel engines rumbled in his brain. The greasy odor from the restaurant next door had assaulted his nostrils and turned his stomach. His duty weapon felt cold in his fist. His voice was thrown to the wind as he had repeatedly called her name.

And then he'd found her.

Slumped on the tarmac behind the truck stop, trying to crawl to her feet, Michele had been moaning softly. He'd dashed to her side, dismayed to find her covered in blood.

Operating on instinct, he'd crouched beside her, ignoring the jagged asphalt chunks cutting into his knees.

He'd gathered her to his chest, cradling her. His fault. If she died, it was all his fault.

She'd cried out when he'd touched her arm, and Nick's heart had cracked into pieces. She was too young, too sweet, too pretty to be faced with this ugly underbelly of life.

He'd risen to his feet, still gripping Michele in his arms, and carried her to the cruiser. An incredible sadness had washed over him. If she died, he would not be able to live with the guilt. It was his sworn duty to protect and defend, and he'd failed her miserably. He'd felt so futile, so useless, just as he had as a small boy, standing helplessly by while his father beat his mother time after time.

Nick had whispered to Michele, telling her he'd never let anyone hurt her again, and then, in a moment of unguarded tenderness, he'd kissed her.

A kiss he regretted to this day.

"Nickerson?"

"Huh?" Nick jerked back to the present and stared at Lieutenant Charboneau.

"Were you listening?"

"Yeah. Sure." Nick ran his hands along his thighs.

"So you concur?"

"Right."

Charboneau looked surprised. "I hadn't expected you to agree so easily."

What had he missed? Nick blinked and looked at Mallory. She was grinning. Uh-oh. Something was up. He'd definitely been daydreaming when he should have been alert.

"No big deal." Nick shrugged, hoping to catch on without admitting he hadn't been paying attention.

"I must say, Nickerson, it's pretty progressive of you to consent to do the cooking while I take over management of the Triple Fork," Michele said. "Truthfully, I anticipated another sparring match with you over this."

"Hold on. Back up. What did you say?"

"You just agreed that I could be the ranch manager at the Triple Fork and you'd take on the cooking and cleaning detail. Weren't you listening?" She folded her arms over her chest and sent him a smug grin.

"Okay, so my mind wandered," he snapped. "You can bet your last dollar I'm not about to do any cooking, that's—"

"I dare you to say, 'woman's work.'"

"I wasn't going to say that." He backpedaled.

"It only makes sense for me to be the manager. I've got experience on a horse farm. You don't."

"Like I have cooking experience?"

"You'll muddle through."

"Lieutenant..." Nick looked back to Charboneau.

"She's got a point, Nick."

"How 'bout we share duties?"

"Why should I? Just because I'm a woman doesn't mean I can cook either."

Nick fought the desire to strangle her. "We're on an investigation. Not playing house."

"Amen to that!" Michele nodded.

"The investigation comes first. Meaning the time spent on the ranch observing the employees and the horses. Am I right?" Nick appealed to Charboneau.

"I'll concede that."

Nick couldn't help thinking that Michele looked so cute when she tilted her head in that haughty manner of hers. "Good. So we'll manage the ranch together?"

"All right. As long as you do the cooking for the stable hands."

"Charboneau," Nick said. "I can't work with this woman. I'll kill her before the day is out."

"Stop it. Both of you," Charboneau growled. "I feel like a kindergarten teacher having to referee you two. Like it or not, you are on this assignment together. Make the best of it."

"Yes, Lieutenant," Nick mumbled.

"Now that we have that settled, you leave tomorrow morning. Here are the keys to the ranch house." Charboneau dug keys from a drawer and tossed them onto the desktop.

Nick and Michele lunged for the keys at the same time. Michele was faster, but before she could claim her prize, Nick clamped his large hand over her smaller one.

Her unexpected softness sent powerful feelings rioting through him. Strangely, Nick felt as if he'd been kneed in the gut. She should not affect him like this, but she did.

They tussled like two bulldogs. Michele clamped her fingers tightly around the keys while Nick attempted to pry them loose.

"Let go," he said amiably, rubbing her knuckles with his thumb until heat sparked up his arm.

"No way. Lieutenant?" Michele turned her big baby blues on Charboneau and batted her long lashes.

"Let go of her, Nickerson," Charboneau interjected.

Nick grunted and released her hand. Michele shot him a sassy look and triumphantly pocketed the keys.

"I want one thing clearly understood," she said.

"What is it now, Mallory?" Nick sighed and rolled his eyes.

"We're equal partners in this investigation. Right?" Michele shifted her gaze to Charboneau. "Neither one of us is over the other?"

An uneasy expression crossed Charboneau's face. "Nick is the senior officer, Michele."

"Yeah, but he doesn't know diddly about horses."

Charboneau glanced at Nick. "What do you say?"

"I outrank her. I should be in charge," Nick said firmly.

Michele shook her head. "If we aren't equal partners then I'm not doing it. Period. It's bad enough I have to pretend to be his wife." She spat out the word as if it were poisonous.

"I'm not comfortable with that. Either I'm in charge, or I'm outta here. That last episode with you proved we can't be equals. Besides, the governor appointed me to the case."

"Stop it!" Charboneau slammed both hands on the desk. His face flushed purple, and the veins on his neck bulged.

Nick and Michele both jumped.

"I don't want to hear any more complaining from either one of you. Got it? Michele, Nick is in charge. But, Nick, you've got to concede to Michele's expert opinion where the horses are concerned. And you'll both share the damned cooking. Is that understood?"

"Gee, Lieutenant, don't have a coronary," Nick said.

"Understood," Michele mumbled.

"Good." Charboneau pulled a white handkerchief from his pocket and mopped his beefy face. "You two could strain the patience of a Benedictine monk."

Nick looked at Michele and grinned.

Her return smile zapped a current of desire clean through his body. A sultry hotness swamped his bones. He gulped. He was in deep trouble here. How long could he live in close quarters with Michele Mallory, pretending to be her husband, before things got completely out of hand?

❦ 3 ❧

By the time Nick rang her doorbell at seven-thirty the next morning, Michele was not only dressed and ready but pacing her small apartment.

She occupied the top floor of a converted Victorian home close to the sprawling campus of the University of Texas. Her unstructured, Bohemian lifestyle at home—in stark contrast to her job with the state police and her strict upbringing— suited her well. From the restaurants farther up the road, delicious aromas spilled out, wafting on the breeze. Musicians and performance artists did their thing on the wide sidewalks amid young couples holding hands or snuggling together. A mix of nationalities rode bicycles or in-line skated or jogged to classes. Michele liked to stroll the streets, breathing it all in, fortifying herself with the energy around her.

She also enjoyed living near enough to see the law school where her father had graduated—the same law school he'd insisted that she attend. Michele had rebelliously refused to follow in his footsteps, had instead selected a career in law enforcement, mostly to irritate Judge Franklin Mallory. But once on the force, Michele discovered she loved her role as a state trooper. She was in control of her own destiny, not her self-righteous father or her obstinate mother.

The doorbell rang again. Trust Nickerson to chafe at the bit. Michele stalked to the door and threw it open.

He stood with one hand on the doorframe, his angular body slouched, a hand cocked at his hip. His gaze swept over Michele, his eyes lingering at the front of her white cotton blouse before sliding lower to inspect the way her faded blue jeans clung to her body.

"I like your hair down like that," he said. "It looks nice, feminine. Not like that uptight French braid you usually wear."

Michele twisted a long lock around her finger. "I was just about to braid it up."

"Leave it."

Despite misgivings, his words thrilled her. Why? What was wrong with her? She always braided her hair, but for some inexplicable reason, today, she did not.

"Here," he said, pulling something from his pocket. "Put this on."

"What is it?"

"Hold out your hand."

Michele extended her hand, and Nick deposited a simple gold band into her palm. "What's this?"

"A wedding band."

"I know *that*. Why are you giving it to me?"

"To give credence to our marriage charade."

Michele stared at the ring, savoring the weight, the metal still warm from his body heat. A strange feeling surged through her. A sensation so weird, she wisecracked, "Oh, gee, what girl wouldn't die to wear Nick Nickerson's ring?"

"Die?"

Fluttering her eyelashes, she slipped the ring onto her finger. It fit perfectly. How had he known her size?

"It's on loan. Don't lose it," he chided, waving his hand.

Michele noticed that a matching band encircled his own ring finger. "Thanks for your confidence."

"Ready?" he asked, ignoring that.

She inclined her head. "You're going dressed that way?"

"What's wrong with the way I'm dressed?" Nick held out his arms and glanced down.

As usual, he looked like a biker in black denim jeans and a black muscle shirt. A small heart was tattooed on his right shoulder, a gold stud earring pierced one ear, and his boots were made for riding motorcycles, not horses. His dark curls were gathered into a small ponytail at the nape of his neck.

"For one thing," Michele said, "that earring has got to go."

"This?" Nick reached up to flick his earlobe. "It's just a gold stud."

"And you'd better lose that ponytail, too. It's completely out of place for a cowboy."

"Willie Nelson has braids."

"Willie's a musician, not a cowboy."

"Okay." Nick removed the earring and stuck it in his front pocket. Then he reached up and pulled the rubber band from his hair in a fluid movement so sexy, Michele hiccoughed against the erotic onslaught.

"You'll need cowboy boots and a hat and some western-style shirts."

"Ah, come on, you really think that's necessary?"

"You're the one with the reputation for being a savvy undercover cop. You tell me."

He stared at her. "You're right. We'll stop on the way, and you can outfit me."

Great. Just what she wanted. Shopping with Nickerson.

"So are you ready?"

"Of course." She waved her hand at the suitcases waiting

beside the door. "I've been up since six. Already put in a three-mile run."

"I got up at five-thirty and did five miles." He smirked and marched over the threshold and into her apartment, his piercing gaze giving her place the policeman's appraisal.

"Bully for you."

"You've got a small apartment," he observed, eyeing her bookcase.

"I'm not home much." She remained standing by the door.

"You actually like living in this hippie neighborhood?"

"It's quite colorful and entertaining."

Nick snorted. "Bet you can get high just smelling the fumes on a windy night."

"I don't recall asking for a critique of my living arrangements."

He walked over to inspect the photographs of Michele and her horse, Thor. "You really are into horses."

"No, I like to pretend. I dressed up in jodhpurs and had my picture taken with a rent-a-horse just to impress people," she said sarcastically, but despite herself, she couldn't help admiring his butt.

The muscle shirt showcased Nick's upper body.

Michele swallowed hard. Although she found him one of the most irritating creatures on the face of the earth, she had to admit she admired his outrageousness. Timid and weak-willed, Nick Nickerson was not.

"Come on now, Mish, no need to be churlish."

"I see you've added a new vocabulary word." How was she going to survive so many days pretending to be his wife? Nervously, she twisted the unfamiliar gold band on her finger.

He picked up one of her riding trophies from the book-shelf. "You're good, too. First place, huh?" His large thumb idly caressed the female rider sitting astride a horse.

Michele's eyes tracked the steady circular movement, and suddenly, she felt lightheaded.

"Can we go?" Michele snapped, trying her best not to think about Nickerson's large thumb massaging her trophy.

"Sure." He returned the trophy to its place and sauntered toward her. Bending, he reached for her bags.

"I can carry my own stuff, thank you very much." Michele slung her carryon over her shoulder and snatched the suitcase from him.

Nick held up his palms and stepped back. "Fine with me."

"We'll take my pickup," she said.

"I'd rather take my car."

Michele rolled her eyes and shouldered past him into the hallway. "Are you still driving that two-seater foreign job?" She set the suitcases down and waited for him to step across the threshold before pulling her door closed and locking it after them.

"Yeah."

"Right. Real smart. Take a flashy car like that to a horse ranch. Anybody with a lick of sense would spot us for a couple of phonies right from the start."

To Michele's surprise, Nick seemed to give her suggestion some thought. She picked up her suitcases again and trotted down the hall, not really caring whether he followed or not.

"Okay," he said, catching up with her as they bounced down the creaky wooden stairs. "We take your vehicle. But I get to drive."

"No way." She glared at him.

"Then we use my car."

"Don't be stupid."

"Ah, come on, be a pal. I hate to ride shotgun." He gave her a come-hither grin, but Michele wasn't falling for it.

"Don't try flattery to get your way, it won't work with me."

"What does work?" He arched an eyebrow and widened his grin.

"Letting me have my way."

They reached the foyer of the Victorian, and Nick opened the door. Michele stepped out into the warm sunlight and deposited her suitcases on the sidewalk. Because it was July, the student population had waned, and pedestrians were unusually sparse.

"Ah, now. This isn't going to work. We both can't have our way all the time," Nick drawled.

"Guess we'll have to learn to compromise."

"Hmm, I suppose so."

"The first compromise, I get to drive," she said firmly.

"Hold on just a minute. The first compromise was we take your truck. Now it's your turn, sweet cheeks. I get to drive." He held out his palm.

"Oh, hell, if it means that much to you." Michele dug in her pocket, then slapped her truck keys into Nick's upturned hand. "You can park your car in my space in the garage. For the record, the next compromise is on you."

"Agreed." He offered his hand.

She shook it.

Merely touching the man shouldn't have caused a riot of emotions to explode in her chest, but it did. Michele jerked her hand away, then spun on her heels. When he didn't follow, she turned around and noticed he had a strange look on his face.

"Well?" she asked. "Are you coming or not?"

"Huh? Oh, yeah. Sure."

They entered the spacious, six-car garage next to the Victorian. Nick backed out her truck out, then moved his red Ferrari into the vacant spot.

A shapely young woman on in-line skates, wearing

nothing but a string bikini, zipped by. She turned her head to stare at Nick and let loose with a loud catcall.

Nick gave Michele a sheepish grin. "Happens to me all the time."

"Poor baby, must be a terrible cross to bear," Michele quipped, but to her dismay, she felt downright jealous. To hide her feelings, she bent to pick up her suitcases off the sidewalk, and tossed them into the back of the pickup, while Nick retrieved his things from the sports car.

"Have you had breakfast yet?" he asked, once they were settled in her pickup.

"No."

"Me, either. Where's the nearest doughnut shop?"

"Doughnuts? Those things will clog your arteries."

"I recall we had this same discussion when we were on stakeout last December," Nick observed.

"Yeah, and you conned me into eating those greasy burgers. Good thing Harbarger shot me when he did, otherwise I would have wasted away of heart disease."

"I take it you're not going to tell me where the doughnut shop is."

"There's a bakery on the corner. You'll have to make do."

He pulled away from the curb with the jerk-neck speed of Mario Andretti. Michele bit down on her tongue to keep from saying something. It would serve him right to get a ticket.

He drove to the end of the block and pulled into the bakery parking lot. The tantalizing scent of fresh-baked bread floated on the early-morning air.

A young man on a bicycle pedaled past them as they got out and emitted a long wolf whistle meant for Michele.

"Happens to me all the time," she said, fluffing her hair for effect.

Nick growled.

Michele ducked her head to hide her smile.

They purchased their breakfast, a Danish and coffee for Nick, and a protein shake for Michele, then made their way back to the truck. A few minutes later, they were barreling down the highway, heading west for Rascal, Texas and the Triple Fork Ranch.

"Okay," Nick said, polishing off his Danish and dusting his fingers on his pants. He drained the coffee and tossed his paper cup on the floorboard. "Let's review this assignment."

Frowning, Michele retrieved the cup and deposited it into a wastepaper sack she kept in the passenger side door. Between her knees, she clutched the protein smoothie. In her lap, she held the manila folder Lieutenant Charboneau had given them the day before.

"What are our undercover names again?" Nick asked.

"Nick and Michele Prescott."

"Our history?" Nick pulled mirrored sunglasses from his shirt pocket and slipped them on. He looked way too cool.

"We're newlyweds."

"Great." Nick tossed her a rakish smile. "This ought to be fun."

"Don't get any ideas, Nickerson. I carry a 9mm Beretta, a stun gun, and pepper spray."

"Gotcha." He chuckled and waved a hand at the folder. "Go on."

"We wanted a job where we could be together. You've done front office work for Manor Downs. And I'm an accomplished horsewoman. At least that part is true."

"How did we meet?"

"At the racetrack. You backed your truck into the side of my horse trailer."

He peered at her over the rim of his sunglasses. "It doesn't say that."

"Yes, it does." Michele held up the paper as proof.

Nickerson frowned. "Makes me sound like a bozo."

"If the horseshoe fits, cowboy..."

"Read me the cast of characters, dear wife."

Michele tried her best to ignore the "dear wife" comment. "The owners of the Triple Fork are Hiram and Myra Branch. Very wealthy. Old oil money. The ranch is basically a tax write-off. According to Charboneau, they're not actively involved in the actual running of the place. That's where we come in, along with their battalion of accountants and lawyers, of course."

The rolling green fields of the Texas Hill Country flashed by the window as they left Austin's urban hustle in the rearview mirror. Various breeds of cattle and horses grazed in pastures strung with barbed wire. On their right, railroad tracks paralleled the highway. Occasionally a small lake shimmered in the distance. In ninety minutes or so, they would be passing through Kerrville and from there, directly into the desert altitude of the Trans-Pecos and the Davis Mountains. The entire trip would take close to seven hours.

"I'm listening," Nick prompted.

Michele slanted him a glance. His tanned hands gripped the steering wheel with supreme confidence. The muscles in his forearms rippled when he moved and flexed. His profile was magnificent—proud, stately, alpha. Physically, Nick Nickerson was the perfect specimen of manhood.

She felt suddenly breathless. Surviving this assignment with her heart intact was going to be much harder than she'd ever imagined.

"Mish?"

"Huh?"

His use of her nickname flustered her. Fighting back a flush of embarrassment at being caught watching him, Michele stared down at the papers in her lap.

"I'm listening," he repeated, a grin spreading across his face.

She cleared her throat. "The last ranch manager and his wife, Lance and Krystal Kane, quit suddenly, walking off the job without notice." She brushed a lock of hair from her forehead. "Wonder if they knew something about the doping?"

"Possibly. Charboneau told me they've been unable to locate the Kanes for questioning."

Michele looked up and met Nick's deep-brown eyes. "Foul play?"

Nick shrugged. "Or they simply don't want to be found."

A shiver ran through her. They were heading into dangerous territory.

"Cold?" Nick's gaze focused pointedly at her chest. Michele glared at him and folded her arms for protection. He reached over and turned down the air-conditioning a notch. "Better?"

Michele nodded. "Currently living at the ranch are James Hollis, the head trainer, age forty-seven." She dampened her finger with her tongue, turned the page, then read off the names of the nine stable hands living at the Triple Fork Ranch.

"No shortage of suspects." Nick pulled a pack of gum from his pocket and offered Michele a piece. The gum's sharp wintergreen scent spiced the pickup's cab.

"No, thanks."

Unwrapping a stick, he folded it into his mouth, favoring Michele with a view of his straight, white teeth. He must have had a good orthodontist. Anybody as arrogant as Nick was bound to have lost a few teeth in bar fights.

"Do you suppose all these people will be living in the house with us?" Michele asked hopefully. If they were surrounded by a houseful of people, it would be easier to resist Nickerson's charms.

"Nope." Nick grinned and popped his gum. "We have our own cottage. I asked Charboneau."

Rats.

"There's more," Michele continued. "They hire lots of part-time day workers to exercise and groom the horses. Most of them are seasonal transients who only work for a few months and move on. And there's the vet, Dr. Richard Felix."

"Ought to be a challenge keeping up with these people."

"Popping in and out on a regular basis are the various horse owners and their families and friends, plus the jockeys. All and all, I'd say we've got about a hundred possible suspects."

Nick whistled. "More complicated than the Harbarger case, eh, Michele? That was simple. We knew it was Harbarger. The only problem was apprehending him."

Why did Nick have to bring up the Harbarger case? Michele winced. Ever since she climbed into the pickup beside him, she'd been fighting the memory of those three weeks spent together.

But despite all the time and closeness, neither of them had revealed anything genuinely personal about their lives. Nick's perusal of her apartment this morning had probably gotten him more info than she'd ever offered herself.

"Well, Nick Prescott, it looks like we have our work cut out for us." Michele closed the folder.

"Yes, *wife*. I'd say you're right."

🦋 4 🦋

Wife.

The word sounded strange rolling off his lips, but kind of nice too.

Hell and damnation, Nickerson, what's the matter with you? Sure Michele Mallory is one hot babe, but don't let that go to your head.

He glanced over at Michele and almost swallowed his gum. She was truly special. Despite her stature, she had the appearance of a fragile china doll—beautiful, burnished-gold locks cascading down her shoulders, wide-set navy-blue eyes that could pierce a man clean through his soul, a peachy-pink mouth just made for kissing.

But, oh, her physical aspects were deceiving. Mentally, emotionally, Michele Mallory was as tough as a pit bull—tenacious, aggressive, determined.

Nick smiled. She reminded him of himself—the woman loved a good scrap. He supposed the paradox of her gentle looks and tough demeanor explained her success as a cop. Criminals, expecting her to be a weak little fluff, underestimated her strength and courage. Nick vowed never to make that mistake.

Not for the first time, he wondered at the past she kept as closely guarded as he did his own. Charboneau had told him Michele came from a wealthy family, but that was all he knew about her.

His own poverty-stricken environment had been quite the reverse of her posh upbringing, yet he sensed similar forces at work in their backgrounds, as if she, too, had experienced a combative childhood where the strong were respected and the weak scorned.

Growing up on Houston's mean streets, Nick could just as easily have become a felon as a law enforcement officer. In fact, he had been on the road to juvenile delinquency until that fateful night he'd forced his father out of the house. He had quickly realized that it was up to him to safeguard the family, and he'd assumed the role of protector with a vengeance.

They drove in silence for a while, Nick maneuvering Michele's vehicle over a well-maintained stretch of Texas highway. He liked her heavy, three-quarter-ton pickup. It was strong and capable, with plenty of staying power, just like the owner.

The cab was immaculately clean. From Nick's view of her apartment this morning, Michele was the particular type. Living in the same house with her ought to be a challenge. Nick prided himself on his lackadaisical cleaning habits. They would clash at every turn.

"Kerrville is up ahead," Nick commented when they passed the road sign.

Michele studied the GPS he'd set. A curtain of hair fell across her cheek, and Nick felt an involuntary tightening just below his belt. Heaven help him, he didn't know how he was going to be able to work side by side with this woman, much less pretend to the world at large that she was his bride.

To carry off the charade, they'd have to do the things newlyweds did—whisper secrets into each other's ears, hold hands, share frequent adoring glances. Nick clenched his jaw. Lieutenant Ray Charboneau was a cruel man.

"Hang a left for the business district," Michele said. "We need to get you some cowboy duds. Look for a secondhand store."

"Secondhand?" Nick complained. The phrase conjured unpleasant images of his mother dragging home clothes from the Salvation Army and Goodwill. Worn, frayed shirts and jeans that smelled of other people. Nick stuck out his jaw. "I want new clothes."

"Nickerson, don't be dumb. You'd look like a tourist playing cowboy in new clothes."

He hated to admit it, but she was right. He'd gone undercover as a hobo once. A cowboy couldn't be much worse. Ignoring the protest of the GPS narrator, he took the next left.

They drove around Kerrville just as the stores were opening for business. Michele found a used clothing store on her phone app, and Nick parked around back.

A tin cowbell tinkled overhead. The store was dimly lit, overstuffed, and musty.

"Howdy!" A round, grandmotherly woman greeted them from behind the counter. Her eyes crinkled merrily at the corners. "What can I do for you folks?"

"My...er...husband's looking for work clothes. He especially needs cowboy boots, well broken in," Michele said.

"I'm sure we can fix you up." The lady gestured. "Men's clothes are along the back wall."

"Your husband?" Nick leaned low, his warm breath tickled

her ear as they made their way past sequined ball gowns and feather boas.

"Might as well get into character now," Michele said, stopping to admire a wide-brimmed women's felt hat.

Nick grabbed her elbow and tugged her toward the back of the store. "No time for browsing. Let's get my clothes and get out of here."

"Typical man." Michele sighed.

"What's that supposed to mean?"

"No patience when it comes to shopping."

"Need I remind you we're on assignment here, not spending the afternoon at Macy's."

"All right, I get the picture." Michele wrenched her elbow away from him and pranced away to where the men's shirts hung.

Muttering under his breath, Nick followed.

"Hmm." She surveyed the thickness of his neck. "What size do you wear? Seventeen?"

"Seventeen and a half."

"Here," she said, taking a red-and-white checkered Western-style shirt from the hanger. "Try this."

"I'll look like a picnic blanket."

"Trust me, it'll complement your dark hair."

Grumbling, Nick stripped off his black muscle shirt.

❧

"WHAT ARE YOU DOING?" MICHELE EXCLAIMED, HER GAZE riveted to his sculpted chest, carved more intricately than any washboard.

"Trying on the shirt like you told me to."

"In the dressing room for pity's sake. What's the matter with you, Nickerson?" She cast a furtive glance over her shoulder. "Talk about calling attention to yourself."

"You think I'm that interesting, huh?" He flexed like a bodybuilder.

"Stop it!" she hissed.

"Ah, come on, Mallory, lighten up. You think that lady hasn't ever seen a man's bare chest before?"

Not a bare chest like this one. Michele gulped. There ought to be a law against a man looking so fine. She stood motionless, trying hard to fight the overwhelming attraction she felt for her partner.

She had to stop thinking like this.

Purposefully, she returned her attention to the clothes in front of her, her mind buzzing with the intensity of a carnival Tilt-A-Whirl. To her relief, Nick snapped the shirt closed over his incredible chest.

Whew. She fanned herself.

He studied his reflection in the full-length mirror. "Not bad."

"Great. Wear it out. Don't you dare expose yourself again."

Nick smirked and wadded his muscle shirt into a ball.

Michele picked out three more shirts, then led him over to the boots.

"This is worse than wearing bowling shoes," Nick complained. "What's wrong with the boots I'm wearing?"

"Nothing, if you want to impress the Hell's Angels. However, since we're going to be on a horse ranch, may I suggest cowboy boots." She snatched a pair off the floor and dangled them at him.

He tried on several pairs and finally found one that fit reasonably well. Next, they shopped around for a cowboy hat. Nick tried on a black Stetson and mugged for the mirror. "Do I look like a real cowboy, li'l lady?" he teased, affecting a John Wayne posture and drawing out his words.

"A straw hat would be more practical," she said matter-offactly, stripping the Stetson from his head and plopping a battered white work hat on his thick, dark hair.

"Ah, but this doesn't suit my image."

"What image is that?"

"The stranger in black."

Michele snorted. "This isn't a spaghetti Western, Nickerson. You're going to be expected to really work on the Triple Fork. Besides, good guys wear white hats."

"Who said I was good?" His eyes sparkled impudently.

Ignoring his innuendo, Michele marched to the cash register. They paid for their purchases and left the store. In a matter of minutes, they were tooling down the interstate once more. Six hours later, they were in the high desert climate of Rascal, Texas.

❦

"How far to the Triple Fork?" Nick asked.

"About fifteen miles," Michele said, tucking a strand of hair behind her perfectly shaped ear and avoiding meeting his gaze.

"Okay, Michele, are you ready for this?" He flashed her his best come-hither smile, but she wasn't buying it. "Newlyweds."

"Ready as I'll ever be to pose as your wife."

"Would that really be such a terrible prospect?"

"Are you kidding? I'd rather get rabies."

"That's honest." But her bluntness stung. Did she really find him so repulsive?

"You ever been married, Nickerson?"

Her question surprised him. When they'd been on the Harbarger case together, she hadn't once asked him a personal question. "Yeah. When I was twenty. It lasted for six months. How 'bout you? Did you ever take the big, till-death-do-us-part plunge?"

"No. And I never plan to get married."

That surprised him. "Why not?"

Michele waved a hand. "Half of all marriages end in failure. Look at yours. I figure, why bother? I save myself a lot of grief."

"Nobody ever asked you, huh?"

Her expression turned haughty. He loved the way she could look like a queen on a throne, ordering servants to do her bidding.

"I'll have you know I've received several proposals of marriage."

"Criminals you've arrested don't count."

"Watch it, Nickerson, I've got pepper spray in my pocket."

Nick's grin widened. Trust Mallory to be prepared for a fight. He liked that about her. Whoever married this wildcat had better know self-defense techniques.

His ex-wife, Julianna, had accused him of the same thing. "You love to fight, Nick," she'd said the day she'd walked out. "And I'm too much of a pacifist to survive marriage with a jungle cat like you."

Yep, he and Michele Mallory were a lot alike. The problem was, put two jungle cats in a cage together, and you got cat soup.

"There's your cutoff," Michele interrupted. She waved at the road sign as they zoomed past. "Next quarter mile."

Immediately afterward, the GPS robot voice said the same thing.

Nick turned on his blinker and changed lanes. Michele lowered the window and drew in a breath of fresh, country air. Her burnished blond hair whipped around her face in an exciting jumble.

Embarking on a dangerous adventure with this gorgeous, high-spirited woman sent a surge of adrenaline skipping through Nick's veins.

Life didn't get much better than this. A good mystery to solve and an intriguing woman at his side. Let him at the Triple Fork!

He was ready to bring fugitives to justice and maybe, just maybe, have a little fun in the process.

NICK LEFT THE HIGHWAY FOR A NARROW FARM-TO-MARKET road, curving across the desert landscape. Following the GPS directions, he drove past a boarded-up gas station and a one-room Baptist church.

"We're are officially in the boondocks," Nick observed. "Charboneau said we're to meet in Marfa every Wednesday at the Dairy Diner."

"They still have those drive-in hamburger joints?"

Nick smiled. "I remember the Dairy Diner in my hometown. That's where I met my first love, Mary Lou Tate. What a tigress. She wore these tight little—"

"Ahem," Michele said. "I'm not interested in hearing about your teenage sexploits."

"Oh, I wasn't a teenager. I was only twelve."

Michele rolled her eyes. "From now on," she said, "I think it's best if we keep our conversation on professional matters."

"But we're newlyweds, dear. We're supposed to share our innermost thoughts and feelings." He fluttered his eyelashes at her. She looked at him as if he'd just announced he had leprosy.

"This is exactly the reason I didn't want to work with you again, Nickerson. You're totally unprofessional."

"Is that the real reason, Michele?" He straightened, and his voice deepened.

"What are you insinuating?"

"I thought maybe it had something to do with that kiss I gave you the night Harbarger winged you in the arm."

"You kissed me?"

"You don't remember?"

Nick looked over. Her face was deadpan. Was she serious? Evidently, she had forgotten the powerful connection their lips had made on that cold, dark night. He sure as hell hadn't.

"I was pretty out of it." Her eyelid twitched.

Ah-ha! She was lying. Feeling self-satisfied, he leaned back against the seat. Nick nodded at the three forks in the road before them. One trailed right, another one left, and straight ahead was a sign proclaiming Triple Fork Stables.

"I hate this undercover stuff," Michele mumbled. "Sneaking around, snooping, having to remember a million lies."

"Really? I thrive on it."

"I'm sure that's why the governor picked you for this project."

"What can I say? I've got friends in high places."

"Political suck-up," she accused.

"I'm good with that. Down and dirty, in your face, Texas political suck-up, babe. I'm going to be a Texas Ranger."

"I believe you've bragged about that on numerous occasions."

"Maybe I'll even run for governor one day."

"Good luck."

"You don't believe I can do it?"

"Nickerson, I believe you can do anything you set your mind to."

"Really?" It pleased him to hear her say so.

"Anyone as arrogant as you is bound to succeed sooner or later."

He navigated the one-lane dirt road, past paddocks filled with Thoroughbreds and quarter horses, palominos and Arabians. He noticed Michele's rapt attention as she oohed and aahed over the beautiful creatures. The scent of horses drifted in on the breeze.

Michele took a deep breath and sighed. "It smells like home."

White wrought iron fencing encased corrals, paddocks, and exercise yards. To their right lay a racetrack complete with starting gates and bleachers. These folks were serious about their racehorses. Nick grimaced. He didn't know much about horses, and he hated being ignorant on any subject. He might have a tougher time than he imagined bluffing his way through this assignment. At least he had Michele on his side to keep him from committing a major gaffe.

Up ahead, the road curved to reveal a collection of buildings. A modern, bright-blue barn, constructed of corrugated metal, dominated the foreground. Four large stables butted up against one side of the barn, and a long shed crouched on the opposite side.

Farther up the hill, a small bunkhouse loomed. A collection of pickups, vans, horse trailers, flatbed trucks, hay balers, and tractors were parked throughout the ranch. A dozen workers scurried to and fro, exercising horses, shoeing horses, and grooming horses.

Nick narrowed his eyes and stroked his jaw with a thumb and forefinger, sizing up the suspects.

"Look," Michele said, in breathless awe. She reached over to touch his arm.

He followed where her finger pointed, moved by the poignant urgency in her voice.

On a hill overlooking the ranch stood a magnificent stallion. The animal was completely black except for a spectacular white starburst on his forehead. He was superbly muscled, the epitome of well-bred horseflesh. At that moment, Nick knew what Michele Mallory loved most in life.

"Oh, Nick." Michele sighed. "Isn't he beautiful?"

Why can't she look at me like that? Nick wondered as he watched Michele's navy-blue eyes take on a dreamy quality.

Where in the hell had that thought come from?

Nick wondered if he was losing it. They were on assignment, and he had better get his dangerous ideas under control. Now. He'd be spending several weeks in close quarters with Michele, and he couldn't afford the luxury of a dalliance. A successful conclusion to this case could come closer to guaranteeing him a place on the Texas Rangers law enforcement team, and he wasn't about to jeopardize that long-held goal for a fling. No matter how pleasant.

No way. No how.

"He's at least seventeen hands." Michele squeezed Nick's arm, and a corresponding contraction tightened his abdomen. "He's unbelievable."

As they watched, the stallion reared up on his back legs and pawed the air.

"Looks pretty wild to me."

"What I wouldn't give to tame him," Michele said, her full attention on the mighty creature.

What I wouldn't give to be that stallion. That wayward thought hurtled through Nick's mind.

"I must admit I'm glad Charboneau forced me to take this assignment," she said.

Me, too, Nick wanted to say but didn't. He stopped the pickup beside the barn and killed the engine.

"You ready, Mrs. Prescott?" He winked at her and grinned. It felt good, sharing this charade with her.

"As I'll ever be, Mr. Prescott. "

﷽ 5 ﷽

T hey got out and walked toward a large paddock where a middle-aged man stood talking to a young woman leading a little girl on a Shetland pony. The man turned to stare at them. He was medium height with a cowboy's angular build, firm jaw, narrow hips, broad shoulders, and rawboned, weather-beaten face. He wore the typical ranch attire—cowboy hat, boots, jeans, and a western shirt.

Nick was glad Michele had insisted he change his clothes.

The man stepped back from the pen and ambled over. "Howdy-do," he greeted them. "Can I help you, folks?"

In the background, the woman and girl watched Nick and Michele with interest. The child, Nick noticed, looked wan, her eyes too big for her little face, her frame too thin for her rounded tummy.

The man extended his hand in greeting.

Nick covered the ground between them. "Howdy. I'm Nick Prescott."

"Jim Hollis." The man pumped Nick's arm. "We've been expecting you."

"Nice to meet you, Jim. This here is my new bride,

Michele," Nick said, quickly slipping into his new role. He reached out and slung his arm around Michele's shoulders and drew her close to him. It felt damned good having her soft skin pressed against his.

"Ma'am." Jim Hollis nodded and tipped his hat. "Welcome to the Triple Fork."

The young woman helped the child off the horse and carried her over to where they stood.

Jim wrapped his hand around the woman's arm. "This is my daughter, Jenna, and my granddaughter, Katie. They came to visit for the afternoon."

"Hi." Michele smiled. "I'm Michele."

Katie shyly buried her head against her mother's shoulder.

"Can you tell Michele your name?" Jenna prompted.

"Katie."

"Well, it's nice to meet you, Katie. How old are you?"

The girl held up four fingers.

"Four years old," Michele exclaimed. "You're such a big girl."

Katie smiled.

"We dropped by for a pony ride," Jenna explained. "Katie was so good at the doctor's office today, so I promised to bring her to see her Pappaw and ride the pony."

Katie looked Michele straight in the eye and placed a tiny hand to her distended belly. "My wiver don't work."

Alarmed, Michele met Jenna's glance.

Jenna nodded solemnly. "Katie has liver failure."

"Oh, I'm so sorry," Michele murmured, not knowing what else to say. Sadness washed over her at the thought of what the little girl must go through. "Can she get a transplant?"

"Not until we can come up with a hundred and fifty thousand dollars." Jenna winced.

"We're gonna get the money." Jim Hollis squeezed his

daughter's arm. "Don't doubt it. That Go Fund Me Page I set up has raised five thousand dollars in two months."

"Thanks, Dad." Jenna smiled faintly, but the look behind her eyes said, too little, too late. "It's time to get Katie home for her nap. Nice meeting you folks." She waved a hand at Nick and Michele and started back across the exercise yard.

"Jim, I'm eager to get to work," Nick said, "but I was wonderin' if you could show us to our cabin first. Wife's got to use the facilities."

Michele frowned. Trust Nick to come up with an excuse that cast her in a bad light.

"Why sure." Jim nodded again. "I understand. Long drive from Austin. The manager's place is on up the road a bit." Jim pointed at the graveled driveway they'd come in on. The road wound past the barn and stables and disappeared over the hill. "Did Hiram give you the keys?"

"He sure did, Jim, thanks. We'll get settled in then be right back."

"Glad to finally have a real cook again, Mrs. Prescott." Jim favored Michele with a smile. "We're getting mighty tired of frozen TV dinners and baloney sandwiches."

"Please, call me Michele," she said.

"Michele it is then."

"Actually, Mr. Hollis, Nick's the cook, and I'm the ranch manager."

Nick gritted his teeth. The scheming little witch. He'd have to keep on his toes around this one.

"Huh?" Jim Hollis's mouth fell open. "Hiram hired a woman manager? Not that there's anything wrong with that. I'm just old-fashioned, I guess."

"What Michele means is that we share duties. We feel like a marriage ought to be a real partnership. Don't we, hon." His grip on her shoulder tightened.

"You bet, babe. "

They smiled at each other like predatory sharks going in for the kill.

"If you'll excuse us, Jim," Nick said.

"Sure. You folks need anything, you just holler." Jim Hollis turned back toward the corral.

"Thanks."

Still gripping Michele's shoulder, Nick propelled her toward the truck. He flung open the passenger side door and practically tossed her inside. Stalking quickly around the pickup, he climbed in and counted to ten before keying the ignition and slipping the truck into gear. Michele sat glaring out the windshield, her arms folded across her chest.

"What's the big idea?" Nick asked, backing out of the driveway and guiding the pickup down the dirt road. "Telling Hollis you were the manager?"

"I wasn't about to let you get away with relegating me to housefrau for a bunch of cowboys, husband dear."

"Did you see the look Hollis gave me? Like I was some kind of a henpecked wimp."

"Ah, does that disturb your fragile male ego? Poor Nicky."

"No. What concerns me is the fact that you almost blew our cover."

"I'll tell you what is much more likely to blow our cover. When you make a fatal mistake about horses, Nick. These guys can smell a drugstore cowboy a mile off. Granted, you're good at playacting, but I thought it was better to make it clear right up front that I was the one with the horse knowledge. That way, when you make a gaffe, it won't seem so outlandish."

"Bull."

"Nick, the party responsible for doping the horses, is going to be on alert. They're expecting an investigation. One slip could get you killed."

"Woman, I was hounding criminals when you were skipping rope in the schoolyard. Don't tell me how to run an investigation."

"I've been a trooper for five and a half years, Nick. I'm not a novice, either, and when it comes to horses, I know what I'm talking about."

"I don't doubt it. I simply feel we should confer before changing any plans."

"Oh, you do, do you?"

"Yes."

Her spicy cinnamon scent filled the cab. Her lips were set in a defiant pout. What an opponent, what a partner, what a woman! With him and Michele on the case, felons didn't have a prayer.

Nick battled a massive urge to reach over, haul her into his arms and kiss her until she begged him to make love to her long, slow, and easy.

He gulped at the racy image blasting through his mind. Michele's lithe body moving beneath his, her high, firm breasts grazing his bare chest. The vision of her limbs entangled sexily with his caused perspiration to dampen his forehead, and a corresponding hotness ricocheted through his groin.

Nick gunned the truck up the hill. He had to stop thinking like this and focus on the job at hand. It was time Miss Michele Mallory learned precisely who was in charge of this investigation.

In the shadow from the mountain was a small frame cottage complete with white picket fence and a neglected vegetable garden. A bedraggled swing sagged on the front porch, held up by rusty chains. Overgrown sagebrush dotted the yard.

Whew. This was the place where they would be sleeping, eating, and sharing the same bathroom for days, weeks, maybe even months to come. He wasn't about to let on to

Michele how that idea affected him. Yes, sir, he was in some kind of trouble.

Nick stopped the truck, rested his forearm on the steering wheel, and glanced over at Michele, trying his best to appear nonchalant. "Honey, we're home."

"Har, har." Michele tossed her head and got out.

Nick ogled her graceful figure. She carried herself like a model—posture perfect, chin in the air like an aristocratic blue blood, completely comfortable in her own luscious skin. He climbed out of the truck and helped her unload the suitcases. Muscling his way up the sidewalk, a bag in each hand, he tried to corral the sexy thoughts zipping around in his sunbaked brain.

"Should I carry you over the threshold?" Nick asked as he set down the suitcases and unlocked the front door.

"Try it, and you'll be picking your teeth up off the floor."

He chuckled. It was going to be an entertaining few weeks.

૭૪૭

MICHELE CHARGED PAST HIM, HER FACE FLUSHING HOTLY. The thought of Nick scooping her into his big strong arms had her pulse pounding. The truth was Nickerson got to her. She had a weakness for incorrigible tough guys, but she wasn't about to let him know it. If he ever discovered her bluster was all bluff, heaven help her.

With one lazy hand, he flicked on the lights, then leaned against the doorjamb, watching her.

Michele stepped across the hardwood floor and tried desperately to ignore the shiver of desire racing through her at Nick's studied perusal. Man alive, but he was deadly with that come-hither gleam smoldering in his dark eyes.

She gulped. Nickerson looked wild, daring, unstoppable.

And she had to pretend to be married to this man! How would she survive the assignment?

Anxious to escape her thoughts and the intensity of Nick's dark eyes, Michele moved around the room. The front door opened into a minuscule living room that housed a worn sofa, a recliner, a coffee table, two lamps, and a small flat-screen TV.

Be it ever so humble.

The living area shunted into the kitchen on the left. Michele walked through it, surveyed the aging appliances, the scarred linoleum, the leaky water faucet, and sighed. She opened the refrigerator. A can of coffee, a stick of butter, and a loaf of bread. Not exactly fully loaded haute cuisine.

"A real starter home," Nickerson said. "But the price is right."

"The place is incredibly tiny," she observed.

"I think the real estate term is cozy."

"Good grief. We won't be able to turn around without bumping into each other." Michele brushed a lock of hair from her eyes.

"Yep." Nick ran a hand along his jaw. "Cozy."

"Cramped is the word I was looking for." Michele breezed past him, and their arms almost touched. She sucked in air, afraid to even breathe. She had to stop reacting like this. Her response was sheer insanity.

"Let's go see the sleeping quarters."

Before she could open her mouth to protest, Nick took her by the hand and hauled her back through the living room and down the narrow hallway.

"What do you think you're doing?" She struggled against his firm grip.

"Looks like there's only one bedroom." Nick nudged open the door with the toe of his cowboy boot, his fingers still clasped around her wrist.

A queen-size bed sat in the middle of the room. The mattress was bare, but it was new, still covered in plastic. A mahogany chest of drawers flanked one wall. A curtainless window overlooked the sun-baked garden.

"Guess you'll be sleeping on the sofa." Michele twisted away from him and broke his hold.

"Wait a minute. Wasn't it your turn to compromise?"

"That's not very chivalrous, making me sleep on the sofa."

"As I recall, you've accused me of being a chauvinist on several occasions. Well, toots, I'm all for equal rights. The sofa is yours."

"You're just determined to get even with me because I told Hollis I was the manager and you were the cook." Michele sank her hands on her hips.

"Maybe." Nick launched himself onto the bed and stretched out. He cradled the back of his head in his palms. "Quite comfy. Of course, you could always join me." He patted the mattress.

"In your dreams, Nick."

"I've got to tell you, Michele, there are women out there who'd give their eyeteeth to be curled up in this bed with me."

"The criminally insane don't count. Nor do little old ladies in nursing homes."

He licked his finger and made a straight mark in the air. "Good one, Mish."

He did look exceptionally magnificent spread out on the bed, his longish hair fanning in coal-black splendor, his biceps bunched enticingly, the hard planes of his chest barely hidden by the Western shirt she'd picked out for him.

"We'll alternate," she said. "One night on the sofa, one night in the bed."

Nick sat up, swung his legs to the floor, and ran a hand through his hair. "You can have the bed."

Michele held up a palm. "No, no. You're absolutely right. We're both law enforcement officers. I should not receive preferential treatment because of my gender."

Nick shrugged. "Okay."

A shaft of disappointment stabbed her. She'd come to expect an argument from Nickerson. His easy acquiescence negated her victory.

"Let's discuss the investigation," he suggested. "Any ideas on how to proceed?"

"You mean you're not going to completely take over and start ordering me around?"

"You've proven yourself a worthy opponent." He smirked. "I'm interested in hearing what you've got to say."

Michele flushed with pride. Did Nickerson really regard her in such high esteem? That was the best compliment anyone had paid her in months. Unless of course, he was just buttering her up.

She narrowed her eyes, trying to decipher his sincerity. "You mean it?"

"Sure. Have a seat, get comfortable." He patted the mattress once more.

Suspicious, Michele eased down on the bed, making sure to keep several inches between them.

"Not a very trusting soul, are you, Mish."

"I'm a law officer, Nick. It isn't my nature to trust."

"Perhaps that's why you've never married."

"What's that got to do with anything?" she snapped, peeved because he'd zeroed in on her weakness. She did have trouble relating to men on an intimate level, probably because so few measured up to her lofty standards. She wanted a man with guts and the moral courage to do what was right despite the odds. So many men seemed to fall short of that ideal. But that was none of Nickerson's business. "I thought we were going to discuss the investigation."

"We are." Nick cleared his throat. "First, I think we should get the lay of the land. As soon as possible, we need to scope out the ranch and meet the cast of characters in this drama."

"I agree."

"We've got to be careful. Don't want to tip our hand. So, from now on, let's agree before we start shooting off our mouths. Okay?" He leaned closer, smelling enticingly of wintergreen.

"We're a team. I know that might be a difficult concept for you but try really hard."

"Difficult for me? Ha! That's the pot calling the kettle black." Nick held up his palms. "I'm the first to admit I like to be in control, but I realize that won't wash with you."

"You've got that right."

"Then we agree?"

Michele shrugged. "I suppose."

Nick stuck out his hand. "Put 'er there, partner."

Bridging the gulf between them, Michele accepted Nick's grip. His firm, capable hand rocked her like an earthquake. Quickly, she dropped her hand and her gaze.

"So, let's get out there and work. I'm sure Jim Hollis is waiting to show us around," she said, trying to hide her embarrassment.

"What do you think of Hollis?" Nick asked, seemingly unaffected by their handshake.

Michele shrugged. "I haven't seen enough of him to form an opinion."

"Ah, come on. Don't give me that. Gut level." He placed a hand to his abdomen, and the seductive notion that ran through Michele's mind definitely should have been censored. "What do you think?"

"Logically, he's a suspect. Maybe the prime suspect."

"Everyone is a suspect. Tell me what you feel."

What did she feel? She felt if Nick were to touch her again, she'd dissolve into a pool of hot, molten lava. She felt like a time bomb waiting to explode. She felt like running her tongue up and down his bare skin until he cried for mercy. Where were these insane thoughts coming from?

Michele shook her head. "I feel sorry for his sweet, little granddaughter. That poor child and her mother. What they must be going through."

"The kid did kind of choke me up," Nick admitted. "But don't let that color your impression of Hollis. Sentiment has no place in a police investigation."

"I don't believe Hollis is involved."

"Actually, I don't think he is, either. Too obvious. But we'll still watch him, anyway."

"Of course."

"I suppose we better go meet the rest of this motley crew." He stood. "Are you coming?"

Michele scrambled to her feet and almost crashed into Nick's chest.

He put out his arm to steady her.

She hissed in air.

His dark eyes gleamed. Michele's stomach did somersaults. Oh, dear! Twin needles of awareness and confusion pierced her skin and clouded her mind. She heard a creaking in the distance, but in her highly sensitized state, the meaning of the sound didn't register.

"Michele," Nick said in an overly loud voice.

Before she knew what was happening, Nick folded her into his arms. He held her so tightly, she feared he could feel her heart thumping through her rib cage.

His rugged face blurred before her. Her head spun. He was going to kiss her.

"Ni—" Michele started to call his name. To warn him, to tell him to stop before she ran for her purse and the pepper spray, but he gripped her shoulders, lowered his head, and welded his lips to hers.

Hard, wild, unrelenting lips that tasted of heated velvet.

He placed a palm behind her head and bent her backward, his tongue running along her mouth with an intensity she'd never believed possible.

His fingers tangled in her hair, and his hips ground against her pelvic bone, stirring inside her a burning so spectacular, Michele thought she might die with longing.

The sensations soaring through her veins were indescribable. Birds sang. Trumpets blared. Fireworks exploded.

This kiss was much different from the one he'd given her in the truck stop parking lot seven months ago. That kiss had been tender, and gentle, seeking to soothe and heal. This experience was so combustible, it deserved a name far beyond "kiss." He plumbed the depths of her, attempting to mine her very soul.

How dare he do this. How dare she allow it!

But her treacherous body absorbed his kiss eagerly. Shocked, Michele realized she wanted him as much as he wanted her.

A door slammed.

Michele jumped and tried to jerk away, but Nick held her prisoner.

"Let go." She struggled against him. "Somebody's in the house."

"Stop it," Nick hissed.

"Oh, excuse me," a voice said from the doorway.

Nick released her so quickly, Michele almost stumbled to the floor. Blinking, she stared at the man standing in front of them. He was about her own age, twenty-six or seven, around five –foot ten. Greasy blond hair flopped over his high forehead. He possessed a weasel-sharp face with a long nose, narrow chin, and squinty eyes, and he grasped a battered cowboy hat in his calloused hands.

"Sorry," he said. "I didn't mean to interrupt you, folks."

Nick raked a hand across his mouth and glared at the guy, acting the role of incensed bridegroom. "We're newlyweds."

Suddenly the whole thing became clear. Nick had known all along this guy was outside. The creaking she'd ignored earlier had been the front porch swing groaning. Had weasel-face been spying on them through the bedroom window?

Damn. Like a good policeman, Nickerson had been on alert while she'd allowed lust to cloud her brain, forgetting, for a brief minute, that they were on a case.

The implication shamed her. Nick had kissed her because of the case, not because he wanted her. Her face flushed scarlet. She should have known better. The disappointment settling into her bones was palpable.

Good grief, what was the matter with her? She should be grateful that Nickerson wasn't interested in her on a personal level. Such an attraction could spell disaster to the investigation and potentially place their lives in jeopardy.

"I'm Steve Bradshaw, head groom. Jim sent me over to see if you were getting settled in." The man smirked and transferred his shifty-eyed gaze to the bed. "I guess you were."

"Nick Prescott," Nick said, shaking the man's hand and ignoring the suggestive gleam in his eyes. "This is my wife, Michele."

"How do, ma'am."

Michele nodded. The guy gave her the creeps.

"You folks ready for a tour of Triple Fork?"

"Sure," Nick said, clasping a hand on Bradshaw's shoulder and affecting a country drawl. "Can't wait to get at them horses."

Michele pretended to smooth wrinkles from her clothes. Her lips still smoldered from the devastation of Nick's mouth. She envied the way he quickly fell into each role. She had a hard time assuming another identity. Nick should have been an actor. He possessed the amazing ability to change personas as easily as teenage girls changed boyfriends.

Had the kiss he'd given her been part of his flawless acting talent? If it was, the man deserved an Academy Award.

And she was the prime candidate for fool of the year.

❧ 6 ❧

I am *Michele Prescott, I am Michele Prescott, I am Michele Prescott,* she repeated to herself as Steve Bradshaw drove them back to the hub of the Triple Fork. This undercover stuff was tricky.

Pressed against the door, Michele was grateful to Nick for sandwiching himself in the middle, so she wasn't forced to sit next to the ranch hand.

"Jim said you two are co-managing the Triple Fork," Bradshaw ventured.

"Yep. My Michele is the real brains of our outfit. She knows horses." Nick reached over, patted her knee, and gave her a conspiratorial wink.

My Michele.

How wonderful that sounded.

He's only pretending affection. Don't take this seriously.

"Hope she can cook, too." Bradshaw chortled. "We got some hungry men on this spread."

"Nick is the chef in the family," Michele said.

"Really?" Weasel-face sent Nick an odd look. "I never

woulda figured a strappin' guy like you would go in for women's work."

Bradshaw knows! Michele panicked. Our cover's blown.

Nick, as if sensing her distress, squeezed her hand. "Guess that's what makes our marriage operate, don't it, hon. We don't believe there's any such thing as men's work or women's work."

Calm down. "That's right."

"This ought to be interesting." Bradshaw parked some distance from the stables. "Come with me, and I'll show you folks around."

Michele knew, from spending time at racetracks as a child, that trucks and cars were not allowed near the stables. Instead, everyone got around on bicycles or golf carts. One could never tell when a rowdy horse might spring loose from his trainer and dash into the path of an oncoming vehicle.

They got out and followed Bradshaw across the yard. The hot Texas sun warmed Michele's scalp as they traveled over the bare earth, their boots kicking up dust clouds. The air smelled of horses. A welcoming aroma. The scent of home.

A spirited iron-gray Thoroughbred harnessed at the manual walker tossed his head and tried to go backward, but the other horses, plodding in a circle, forced the spirited animal to conform. The gelding fought and kicked but to no avail.

Michele eyed the high-strung horse and wondered if he was naturally nervous or if something had upset him.

Willie Nelson's nasal twang blared from the speakers of someone's MP3 player. It had been too long since she'd been around horses. Occasionally, she rode with friends at the stables in Austin, but those sad nags could not compare with the feel of a fine, lean-muscled animal between your legs.

At that thought, she peeked over at Nickerson.

He and Bradshaw were chatting like long-lost friends.

Nick had one finger looped through his belt buckle in a cocky stance. His ebony hair curled seductively around his ears.

She caught a glimpse of the scar on his jaw and wondered, not for the first time, how he'd earned it.

Stop it, Michele, she scolded. Nickerson was the hunkiest thing on two legs, but big deal. He was also an egotistical, take-charge jerk who reminded her way too much of her father. *Don't you dare let him get under your skin.*

Bradshaw pushed open the door, and they stepped through into the most modernized livery that Michele had ever seen. The equipment was new, the sawdust fresh. The stalls were immaculate with stable boys scurrying to and fro, carrying pitchforks or shovels or buckets and brushes.

Her mother would have been impressed. Virginia Mallory had insisted on spotless quarters for her horses. Michele supposed that was where she'd inherited her tendency for excessive neatness.

The vented roof and overhead fans allowed air to circulate inside the barn, keeping the place cool despite the sweltering sun outdoors. Ten box stalls lined the walls with two more rows down the middle.

Sparrows flitted through the open rafters. Curious horses peeked over the stalls at the visitors, some nibbling at hay swinging from the slings mounted on pegs outside the doors. One spindly-legged mare who looked to be no more than two gnawed at a thick rope.

The previous ranch manager deserved a lot of credit. No wonder the Triple Fork had a stellar reputation. Boarding wouldn't come cheap. Charboneau believed that the owners, Hiram and Myra Branch, had nothing to do with the race-horse dopings, but Michele wasn't convinced. Anyone putting up this kind of money would be looking for either a guaranteed return on investment or an enormous tax write-off. She made a mental note to discuss this with Charboneau when they met on Wednesday.

Bradshaw guided them past the stalls, calling out the names of the horses as they went. Some of the animals were quite renowned in racing circles.

"Day help," Bradshaw grunted when Nick asked him how many stable hands the Triple Fork employed. "We got anywhere from fifteen to twenty, depending."

Michele stopped to scratch one friendly Thoroughbred's silky nose and resisted an urge to ride. Nick and Bradshaw kept right on walking, and she had to hurry to catch up with them as they passed from the stable into the adjoining tack room.

Saddles, bridles, blankets, ropes, grooming brushes, and feed buckets hung from pegs on the sturdy cedar walls. The room smelled distinctly of rawhide and sawdust.

Home, Michele thought again. *Home.*

A flash of memories floated through her mind. Riding bareback across the prairie. Flying over the fallow fields, wild and free on Thor's broad back. Beautiful memories that made her long for bygone days. But darker memories were lurking in the past, as well.

Michele recalled her mother, strong and domineering, instructing her on how to curry a horse. She would stride up and down the stables, her blond hair held perfectly in place by a tight ponytail, occasionally striking her crop against her gloved palm for emphasis as she barked out orders.

Her father, equally as bossy, would come along a few minutes later and issue conflicting instructions. Then a loud, verbal argument would ensue between the two of them, and Michele would run for cover, usually seeking refuge with Thor. Life in the Mallory household had often resembled an emotional war zone. One never knew when a mortar attack would erupt.

Michele supposed that was where her need for control

originated. Growing up with determined, headstrong parents who had constantly bickered had shown Michele how disagreements were conducted—noisily and frequently.

She still remembered the first time she'd gone against both parents. Her mother had pushed her toward a career in horse racing while her father had insisted she become a lawyer and then a judge. Defiantly, Michele had become a cop, shocking them both. She smiled to herself, recalling that sweet victory. At last, she'd done something only for herself, and it had felt like freedom.

Just like her parents, she and Nick Nickerson were too much alike. And just like her parents' failed marriage, any relationship between them was doomed to end in disaster.

"Michele?" Nick prompted.

"Huh?" Michele blinked and looked up at Nick and Bradshaw. They stared at her expectantly.

"Steve asked if you'd be interested in seeing the training area."

"Oh, yeah, sure. Let's go."

❦

THEY LEFT THE SHADED COMFORT OF THE STABLES FOR THE radiant afternoon heat. Michele's stomach rumbled, and she realized she hadn't had food since the protein smoothie.

"This here is the first paddock," Bradshaw said, stopping outside a small fenced area. "We use it as a holding pen while loading horses into the trailers. You'll see it in action come Thursday when we get ready to take the animals up for the weekend races in Austin at Manor Down's."

Two men stood inside the enclosure. One held a skittish mare by the bridle, tilting her head back, while the other man, robed in a white lab jacket, peered down the horse's mouth with a lighted instrument.

"Hey, Doc, come meet our new managers," Bradshaw called out.

Steve opened the gate and motioned Nick and Michele inside. "Dr. Felix is the Triple Fork's vet."

The man in the white lab jacket looked up. He pocketed the instrument and stepped away from the mare. Smiling, he approached.

"I'm Dr. Richard Felix," he said wiping his hands on a green towel draped over the paddock fence.

"Nick Prescott," Nick replied. "And this is my wife, Michele."

"How do you do?" Dr. Felix shook hands with them both. "Welcome to Triple Fork." He met Michele's gaze, and his smile widened. "If I may be so bold, you're very pretty, Mrs. Prescott."

"Thank you," she said stiffly. Michele didn't like the guy. Not one bit. The word unctuous came to mind. The way Nick held his shoulders straight, alert, she knew he felt the same. Michele forced a smile when she longed to tell the pompous doctor what he could do with his compliments.

Down girl. She could almost hear Nick voice the words.

Startled, she glanced at him. He raised an eyebrow and shrugged. It was uncanny, the way they picked up on each other's vibes.

"I hope you'll enjoy your new job," Dr. Felix said. "It was quite a pleasure to meet you both, but I must get back to my work." He indicated the mare with a wave of his hand.

"What's wrong with her?" Michele asked, assessing the Thoroughbred.

"Bella's off her feed. I'm placing her on a high-protein, megadose vitamin regime twice daily."

"What kind of vitamins?"

"B6, beta-carotene, E, A, and of course C. It also contains

trace elements and protein supplements. It's a formula I created myself, and the horses respond very well."

"Is Bella racing?" Michele asked, curious about the potion Dr. Felix was feeding the mare. Could he be involved in the doping? Logically, a vet could get away with a lot more than anyone else at the stables.

Dr. Felix shook his head. "She foaled four weeks ago. Unfortunately, the colt died."

"Maybe that's the problem," Michele said. "She's in mourning."

"If you'll excuse me." Dr. Felix looked at her as if she were nuts. He gave a curt nod and moved away.

Bradshaw ushered them out of the paddock to finish their tour. He showed them the remaining corrals, the exercise yards, and the practice track, which was in the process of being resurfaced. As they made their way around the ranch, he introduced them to farriers, trainers, and jockeys.

"Tell me about that black stallion I saw when we arrived," Michele said, once they'd completed the rounds and ended up back at the barn where they'd started.

"You'd be meaning Jet." Bradshaw grinned. "He's some kind of ornery."

"Wild?"

"Does a bear—oops," Bradshaw shook his head, chagrined, and interrupted his colorful slogan. "Sorry, Mrs. Prescott. Yeah, Mr. Jet's real wild. Only a few can ride him. Not me. Tosses me in nothing flat. Hiram can ride him and Jim. That's about it."

I bet I could, Michele thought. What a challenge that massive stallion presented.

"Maybe your husband would like to give Jet a try some-time." Bradshaw snaked a subversive glance at Nick. "He looks like he could handle horseflesh."

Despite the hot afternoon, a chill chased over Michele.

What did Bradshaw mean by that remark? Had he guessed Nick was unfamiliar with horses?

A troubled expression crossed Nick's face. Was he afraid? Big bad Nick Nickerson? Probably smart of him. If he didn't know anything about horses, a stallion like Jet would grind him to hoof powder in nothing flat.

"I think running this ranch won't give me time to cavort with wild stallions, Steve." Nick slapped Bradshaw on the back as if he hadn't recognized the veiled threat. "But thanks for the offer."

Jim Hollis waved at them and loped over. "What do you think of Triple Fork?"

"Impressive spread." Nick nodded.

"Isn't it?" Jim beamed pride for the ranch on his weather-beaten face. "I don't mind telling you, Prescott, I was a bit disappointed when Hiram told me he was going outside for a new manager. I kinda hoped I'd get the position."

Oh-ho. Conflict. First Bradshaw, now Hollis. Both men wanted to butt heads with Nick. Michele surveyed the three men standing in front of her and tried to size up the dynamics of the situation. How would Nickerson handle them?

Nick leaned close to Hollis and winked. "I'll let you in on a secret, Jim, if you promise not to tell Hiram Branch."

He's good, Michele thought. Real good. Nick knew "secret" was a magic word.

Hollis looked at Bradshaw. "Ain't you got something to do, Steve?"

The weasel-faced man frowned. "What? You sending me off like an errand boy?"

"Steve," Hollis barked sharply.

Angrily, Bradshaw turned on his heels and stalked off.

"You were saying?" Hollis returned his attention to Nick.

Nick dropped his voice. Michele had to strain to hear.

"This job is temporary for us." Nick nodded his head at her. "Michele wants babies and a home. We're just doing this until we can afford our own spread."

Hollis looked relieved. "Well, thank you, Nick, for saying so. Gives me hope, if you know what I mean."

Nickerson had turned a potential foe into an ally. "Please don't let on to Hiram. I don't think he'd have hired me if he knew we weren't planning on staying long. Especially after the episode with your last manager."

"He told you about that?" Hollis sounded surprised.

"Not much. But enough."

Boy, Nickerson could charm his way out of a paper bag. Michele rolled her eyes and crossed her arms. Was she the only person on the face of the earth who didn't fall for his cock-and-bull strut?

"Could I speak to you confidentially?" Hollis cast a glance in Michele's direction.

"Why sure, Jim," Nick said.

Heads down, they strolled a distance away from her.

She didn't like this. Not one bit. What were they up to? She was part of this investigation, and Nickerson had no right to exclude her. Michele almost marched over to them but stopped herself. Now wasn't the time to make an issue, but just wait until she got Nickerson alone.

The two men talked for a few minutes, then Nick nodded and walked over to where they'd left Michele.

"It's feeding time." Nick tapped his watch.

"Oh?"

"They start rounding up the horses at five."

"Then let's get to work."

"Uh, there's a slight problem."

"What?"

"The ranch hands eat at seven."

"So?"

"Somebody needs to start supper."

"This isn't fair, Nick."

"Keep your voice down."

She glared at him. How like a man! Shunting her off to kitchen duty, even after Nickerson had promised her he wouldn't.

"It isn't me, Michele. Hollis said the help was grumbling about you being the manager. Seems you being a woman intimidates them."

"What!"

"Shhh."

"I know ten times more than you do about horses, but that means nothing?" Michele lowered her voice to a harsh whisper. "I can't believe this small-minded, backwater attitude."

"Sorry, honey. Everybody isn't as enlightened as I am."

"Don't you dare 'honey' me, Nick. I am a professional law enforcement officer and a grown woman."

"Why don't you just get a megaphone and announce to the whole staff that we're not getting along?" Nick hissed, wrapping his fingers around her arm and squeezing firmly. "Now get a grip on your temper. I won't have you jeopardizing this job. Charboneau put me in charge, and you'll do as I say."

Michele was furious. "You'll pay for this underhanded dirty dealing, Nick. And that's a promise."

Relegate her to the kitchen, would he?

Well, she'd fix Nickerson's wagon. And while she was at it, she'd educate those other chauvinistic cowboys as well. After this meal, they'd be begging for frozen TV dinners.

7

Determined, Michele rifled through the bunkhouse pantry, slapping supplies on the counter. Yes, sir, they'd never ask Michele Mallory to cook supper again.

Underneath the cabinet, she unearthed a cast-iron kettle and slammed it onto the aged gas range. One-up her, would he? Not bloody likely. Nickerson might be the senior officer in charge, and she had to obey his orders, but she certainly didn't have to cook well.

Muttering under her breath, Michele tore open the plastic wrap from around a ten-pound package of hamburger meat and dumped it into the kettle. She followed that with six cups of uncooked rice, two quarts of water, and a whole jar of jalapeno peppers.

The door creaked opened. Michele took a step backward and inclined her head to see who was coming inside.

A tiny, young woman dressed in brightly colored jockey regalia stepped over the threshold, unsnapped her helmet, and stuffed her riding crop into her back pocket.

"Hi!" the girl said breathlessly, her face ruddy from recent exercise.

"Hello," Michele said, realizing this was the first female she'd seen on the grounds of Triple Fork besides Jenna and Katie.

The girl took off her helmet and tucked it under her arm. She pulled off her leather riding gloves, and walked across the kitchen, extending her hand. She didn't look much older than twenty-one.

"I'm Elvira Montrose, welcome to the Triple Fork."

Michele wiped her hands on the seat of her jeans and accepted Elvira's handshake. Elvira was around four foot eleven. Standing beside the petite woman, Michele felt like an awkward giraffe.

"Michele Mal... Prescott," she said, correcting herself quickly. "I just got married," she explained to cover her blunder, "and I'm not quite used to my new name."

"Oh, I understand." Elvira grinned. "After husband number two, I decided to keep my maiden name for good. It's such a hassle to keep changing your driver's license and social security card. I don't even know why we're supposed to take a man's name. Far as I'm concerned, we should keep our own right from the start or let men take our name. Turnabout is fair play, I say."

Amen, sister.

"How many times have you been married?" Michele asked, instantly liking the breezy little jockey. If she'd been married twice, surely, she was much older than she looked.

"Just kicked number three out the barn door." Elvira's gray eyes twinkled.

Michele raised an eyebrow but didn't comment.

"I know. Why on earth do I keep taking the plunge? Hey, if I knew the answer to that, I'd be happily single for the rest of my life. Unfortunately, I'm an incurable romantic, and I love these no-account horsemen," Elvira chattered gaily. "But I guess I don't have to tell you. I met that hunky husband of yours, and I just had to come in and say hi. By the way, if you ever get tired of him, just throw him in my direction. I'd catch him in a split second."

Michele longed to tell Elvira she was welcome to Nickerson and good riddance.

"My," Elvira said, fanning herself with a hand. "I haven't seen pecs like that on a man since the last Jason Momoa movie. I bet your hubby is good in the sack, eh?"

Michele's mouth dropped at Elvira's brashness.

"I know." Elvira giggled. "Rude question."

Michele felt jealous thinking about hot-to-trot Elvira out there sizing up her man. *Her* man! Good gravy. Where on earth had that thought come from?

"There's not much to do around here but work and gossip, although Rascal is not quite as calm as it seems. A couple of years ago, a murderer escaped from Huntsville and hid out at a local dairy farm at Christmas. Then a while back, there was a rash of cattle thefts. Plus, the owner of the ranch next door, Kurt McNally, was engaged to the actress Elizabeth Destiny, but they broke up."

"Elizabeth Destiny? I love her movies."

"Me too, but she's not a very nice person. Good thing Kurt found that out in time. He's a terrific guy." The look on Elvira's face said she wouldn't mind a bit being Kurt's new woman. "So how did you and Nick meet?"

"I was racing a three-year-old quarter horse at Trinity Meadows, and Nick accidentally backed his pickup into my trailer," Michele ad-libbed, embellishing the bare-bones history Charboneau had provided.

"Your man is certainly a honey. He could run over my

horse trailer anytime. Unless of course, my horse was inside. He didn't hurt your horse, did he?"

"No." Michele grinned. Despite her fascination with men, Elvira was a true horsewoman, just like Michele's mother. With such women, horses would always come before men, no exceptions.

Elvira walked over to the stove, her boots echoing on the hardwood floor, her helmet still tucked beneath one arm. "Whatcha cookin'?" she asked, lifting the kettle lid and standing on tiptoes to stare down at the mush simmering there.

"Hamburger surprise."

Elvira raised her head, a startled expression on her pleasant face as she replaced the lid. "Boy, that is a surprise. I usually brown my meat first."

Michele shrugged. "I don't know how to cook," she admitted truthfully. Growing up in a household run by hired servants had not prepared her to assume domestic duties. She'd never once seen her mother cook anything with her own hands.

"Why'd you take a job as a cook?" Elvira asked.

"To be with Nick."

Elvira shook her head, her springy auburn curls bouncing. "I hear you. Love will make you do some strange things."

"But I'm good with horses, too," Michele explained, continuing to fabricate the story as she went. She'd fill Nick in on the details later. "That's why Mr. Branch agreed to hire us as co-managers. Problem is, somebody's got to do the cooking, and Nick tricked me into it."

"Well," Elvira said. "Maybe I could give you a few basic pointers. 'Course, it's not like I'm the best cook in the West. I make things that take the least amount of fuss and muss."

The petite woman deposited her crop, helmet, and

leather gloves in the seat of a kitchen chair, then unsnapped her jacket and wrested out of it.

Rolling up her sleeves, Elvira went to the sink and scrubbed her hands to the elbows.

"I think we can salvage this dinner yet."

Michele wasn't sure she wanted the dinner saved. In her mind, she'd been enjoying the image of Nickerson's dismayed face when he tasted the wicked brew she'd been whipping up expressly for his discomfort. But it was kind of Elvira to pitch in, and it gave Michele the opportunity to quiz the other woman about the Triple Fork.

"Now," Elvira said. "We'll just add some stewed tomatoes, onion, garlic, and bell peppers."

Michele arranged the ingredients on the cabinet while the other woman set to work. "How long have you riding out of the Triple Fork?"

"Me? About eighteen months. I started after I moved down here from Oklahoma. Back home, I was mainly riding on bush tracks."

"Running match races?" Michele raised an eyebrow at Elvira's reference to the illegal practice of racing horses against each other on small farm tracks for high-stakes wagers.

"Yeah. But hey, I was a kid trying to get experience. Like every other jockey, I wanna make it to the Derby someday."

Michele knew all about that dream. She'd wanted to follow in her mother's footsteps and become a jockey herself. But nature had played a cruel trick, and she'd inherited her father's tall genes. Even though for her five foot nine frame, she was slender at a hundred and twenty-five pounds, she was still too heavy to be a successful jockey.

"Did you know the previous manager and his wife?" Michele asked, searching the unfamiliar kitchen drawers until she found a paring knife.

"Yeah. You sure put a lot of jalapenos in here," Elvira observed, stirring the hamburger surprise. "But it should be okay. You know cowboys. They like hot and spicy." She grinned unabashedly. "Maybe that's why they're so attracted to me."

"What happened to the other managers? When Mr. Branch hired us, he said they left without warning."

Elvira crinkled her pert little nose. "That's all I know. One day they were here. The next day they were gone. Nobody saw them leave."

"Kind of mysterious, isn't it?" asked Michele, busily chopping two onions.

"Naw. Not if you knew Lance and Krystal Kane. They never could stay put."

"So their disappearance really didn't seem out of the ordinary."

Elvira twisted her neck up to meet Michele's eyes. "How come you wanna know?"

Michele shrugged. "Just interested in what happened to the folks who managed the ranch before us. I figure it would help to know what went wrong, so Nick and I don't make the same mistakes."

Elvira bit her bottom lip as if she were about to say something but caught herself. Instead, she tossed the chopped onion into the mix and opened three cans of stewed tomatoes.

"Elvira?"

The girl shifted her weight. "Look, it's none of my business what was going on between Lance Kane and Steve Bradshaw. But if I were you, I'd avoid those friends of Steve and their crazy schemes."

"I don't understand." Michele stopped peeling the garlic clove and stared at Elvira. "What friends? What schemes?"

"Never mind. Forget I said anything."

"Is something illegal going on at the Triple Fork? They're not running match races here, are they?"

Elvira cleared her throat. "Do you know how to make cornbread?" she asked, evidently determined to change the subject.

Michele longed to press the jockey for more details, but she didn't want to rouse her suspicions. She couldn't risk blowing their cover. Resigned, she dropped the line of questioning. "Nope, never made cornbread in my life, but if you tell me how, I'll see if I can follow your instructions."

Forty-five minutes later, the aroma wafting from the kettle smelled downright delicious while the cornbread toasted golden brown in the oven. Michele's empty stomach was more than grateful for Elvira's intervention with the supper preparations.

"Wanna taste?" Elvira asked, dishing up a small portion on a saucer. The rice had cooked up fluffy with the meat and vegetables into a casserole consistency. Tentatively, Michele took the fork Elvira offered and dipped it into the mix.

"Hmm, not bad," she admitted, savoring the spicy tang that brought Cajun cooking to mind. "Thanks a lot, Elvira, I don't know what I'd have done without you."

"Make a lot of cowpokes mad," Elvira answered honestly, grabbing a pot holder and slipping the huge pan from the oven. "Looks like you did good with your first attempt at cornbread."

"I'll set the table," Michele volunteered.

The kitchen was adjacent to a large dining room. Three unvarnished pine tables were lined in a row, each seating eight. Michele found dishes and napkins in the cupboard, and Elvira brewed fresh tea and coffee. While laying out the silverware, Michele couldn't stop thinking about what Elvira had said.

Steve Bradshaw was up to some crooked scheme, she just knew it. Michele had mistrusted the man on sight, and with good reason, it seemed.

The back door opened, and Nick stepped inside. At the sight of him, Michele's heart stuttered in her chest. The memory of the kiss he'd given her back in the cottage slammed into her mind, haunting her with an unexpected vengeance.

Heavens, he had tasted so darned wonderful. Good thing the kiss had been to establish their cover for Steve Bradshaw's benefit. If Nick had really meant that kiss, well... Michele didn't even want to entertain that thought.

Elvira turned away from the kitchen sink, where she was freeing ice cubes from a plastic tray and focused her adoring eyes on Nickerson.

"Hello, Mr. Prescott," she chirped, courteous and friendly.

Far too friendly to suit Michele.

"Please, call me Nick," he said, turning on his hundred-watt smile.

Elvira giggled. "And, please, call me Elvira."

"My pleasure, Elvira," Nick replied, his gaze flickering over the jockey to settle on Michele standing in the dining room.

Michele's breath hung suspended as she absorbed the intensity of Nick's stare. A five o'clock shadow ringed his solid jaw, cloaking all but the top of his silvery scar.

Dust and dirt decorated his clothing. Straw clung to his coal-black curls. His face was flushed from hard work in the hot, Texas sun. The perspiration riding his brow heightened his rugged appeal.

The man was a powerhouse—dynamic, vital, alive with pure sexual energy. He exuded unmistakable masculinity that shook Michele to her toes.

Gulping, she tried to dispel her errant thoughts.

Speculating on those things could only lead to trouble. After all, she had to spend the night alone with him, and the memory of that earth-shattering kiss kept playing over and over in her mind.

It was going to be a very long night.

8

"I came to see how you were doing," Nick said, his eyes never leaving Michele's face.

"Dinner's ready." She met his stare and raised her chin.

"Boy," Elvira said. "You two have it bad for each other, huh?"

"Could you excuse us?" Nick asked, turning to Elvira. "I'd like to speak to my wife in private."

Elvira waved a hand. "Go right ahead. Smooch away. I'll be back in a minute." She let herself out, closing the back door firmly behind her.

"Wonder what she meant by that." Michele laughed nervously. Nick looked downright predatory as he moved across the kitchen toward her.

"Got me," he said, but Michele could tell he felt the same zinging response surging through his veins. Had they been apart two hours? It seemed like a decade.

"Dinner's ready," she said again, not knowing what else to say.

He moved closer. She wanted to take a step back, to get

away from his eagle-eyed stare, but quelled the urge. She refused to show fear.

"So you said." Nick stood inches in front of her, his hip cocked at a provocative angle, the folds of his denim jeans accentuating his natural attributes.

Michele tried hard not to notice, but despite herself, she felt her gaze drawn down, down, down to where the seams strained white. Man-oh-man-oh-man. She swallowed, and looked up to meet his eyes again.

"I better butter the cornbread," she said, using the first excuse that came to mind. Anything to wedge a safe distance between them.

"Not so fast." Nick propped an arm against the counter, blocking her exit.

"Nick..." she said, trying to think of a haughty retort and failing miserably. "You assigned me to kitchen duty. Let me finish my chores."

"Stop being so hardheaded for one minute, Mish. I'm trying to apologize."

"What?"

"You were right," Nick said.

"Oh? About what?"

"About the horses. About being ranch manager."

"Yes? Go on."

He held up his hands. Blisters covered his palms, his fingertips.

She winced.

"I thought I was in pretty good shape," he said. "I jog five times a week and work out with weights every other day. To tell you the truth, I didn't know wrangling horses could be such exhausting work."

Michele placed a hand to her forehead and pretended to swoon. "Catch me," she said, "I think I might faint. Nick Prescott admits to having faults."

"A mistake," he growled. "I'm admitting one mistake."

"Call the media, stop the presses, get your phones to record this monumental occasion."

"Sarcasm becomes you."

Michele beamed. "Thank you."

Nick's mouth twitched. "We're not doing too well with our assignment. A horse ranch manager who doesn't know horses and a cook that can't cook."

"And you thought you were just going to breeze in and absorb the essentials of horse training through osmosis."

"It's worked for me in the past."

"I love it," Michele said. "The great Nick Prescott has met his Waterloo, and it is horses."

The back door creaked open, and Elvira poked her head in. "You guys done doing the wild thing yet? Me and the boys are starving.

Michele laughed and waved them inside.

This was a no-frills bunkhouse, much less elaborate than the place on her parents' ranch. There was a kitchen, a big dining room, and a row of bunks at the back of the house. Michele had noticed a worn vinyl sofa in the corner of the back room and a TV on a nightstand. But most of the ranch hands had little time for relaxing.

Spurs jangled against the wooden floor. The room filled with the smell of horses, leather, and saddle soap. Michele took a quick head count, saw they had fifteen for supper. Hoping she'd made enough food, she took bowls from the cabinets and started dishing up the casserole while everyone laughed and joked and crowded into the kitchen around her.

One cowboy was singing "Elvira," while affectionately tweaking the jockey's short curls.

"Shut up, Eddie," Elvira said good-naturedly and swatted the cowboy's hand away.

"Mmm," someone else commented. "Smells heavenly."

"Whatcha cooking?" Yet another lanky cowboy wandered over and stuck his nose over the kettle.

"Here," Michele said, thrusting a brimming bowl of food at the inquisitive cowpoke. "Go sit down."

"Hey, little miss." He grinned, wrapping a big paw around the bowl and took a muffin from the platter piled high with cornbread. "You gonna fit right in here. You can call me Justin." The cowboy favored her with a slow wink.

"And I'm Mrs. Prescott," she said, glad for the first time since assuming this assignment that Charboneau had insisted she and Nick go undercover as husband and wife. Surely, not one of these cowboys would be foolish enough to tangle with Nick.

The cowboy nodded. "Yes, ma'am." He cast a sheepish glance in Nick's direction before ambling over to a table.

Michele couldn't resist sneaking a peek at Nick. He stood against one wall, muscular arms folded over his chest, his black eyes blazing a hole straight through her.

He's jealous, she thought, thrilled. But why should he be jealous? Not a single man in the room could compare to him.

No one else possessed that dangerous, untamed look, although she suspected Steve Bradshaw courted such an image. But Nick's demeanor wasn't something that could be manufactured. He merely was potent, unbridled, wild. He could just as easily have been an outlaw as a lawman, owning the essential qualities for either role—bold, domineering, ruthless when necessary.

Michele dished out more food, her body on constant alert. She could feel the heat of Nick's stare. He was supposed to be watching the ranch crew, alert for potential suspects, not scrutinizing her every move.

"Thank you, Mrs. Prescott." One of the younger stable hands accepted his bowl and scurried away.

The noise level rose as one by one the cowboys accepted

their bowls and found their seats. The talk centered solely on horses. Who was sick, who was racing well, who might benefit from various treatments. Michele took it all in and smiled.

My, how she'd missed the easy camaraderie of ranch life. As a child, she'd spent more time with the hired help than with her own parents. The bunkhouse had always been a friendly, inviting place as opposed to the pristine environment of the Mallory six-bedroom mansion.

How could she have stayed away from the racing life for so long? Even though the family homestead had been sold when her parents divorced, Michele had never lost her love for the outdoors and horses. Maybe after this assignment was over, she could get a permanent position working security at a racetrack somewhere.

Father would love that.

Michele squelched the childish thought and dished up another bowl of the hamburger concoction. Head down, Michele turned to the next cowboy in line and plowed straight into Nickerson.

"Oh," she exclaimed, her breath escaping in a little gasp as their elbows connected.

She didn't want to look into those coal-black eyes, but darn it, she couldn't help herself. An intoxicating half-smile quirked his lips.

His sultry gaze nailed her to the spot more securely than a farrier's nail in a horseshoe.

"Here you go," she said, trying hard to breathe through her constricted airway. Why did Nickerson affect her so viscerally? When he stared at her, she felt it clean through to her marrow.

"Thank you," he said. Then he took the bowl and moved toward the table, leaving Michele suddenly bereft, as if all color had been drained from the universe.

This is ridiculous, Michele Lauren Mallory, she scolded herself, scraping the last of the hamburger glop into the remaining bowl. *You have got to stop thinking like this. You're a professional. You cannot let emotions override common sense. Remember the Harbarger assignment? If you hadn't been trying to impress Nickerson with the arrest, you wouldn't have gotten shot.*

Michele squeezed in next to Elvira, straddling the bench across from Nick. Determined to fight the growing attraction she felt for the man, Michele pointedly kept her eyes focused on her food.

"Yum, this hamburger stuff sure is good, Mrs. Prescott," Eddie Ventnor exclaimed.

"Sure is," Jim Hollis chimed in. "Real spicy, just like I like it."

The other hands murmured their pleasure as well.

"Actually, El..." Michele began.

Elvira kicked her under the table and shook her head. Michele caught her meaning.

"It's an old family recipe," she finished, touched by her new friend's kindness.

"Well, it's a good 'un."

"Thanks." Elvira had worked wonders with the mess, rescuing her vengeance recipe with the creative use of spices.

Conversation resumed, and Michele happily contributed to the discussion. She felt disloyal, knowing these kind folks had accepted her so readily as one of their own. She was here to spy on them, and Michele hated to betray their trust. Could any of them really be involved in racehorse doping?

❦

NICK WATCHED MICHELE INTERACTING WITH THE cowboys and tried hard to ignore the stab of jealousy flashing through him. She did look at home here, sweetly brushing off their flirtations. He felt out of place, and Nick hated that feeling.

If his miserable childhood had taught him anything, it was to always assume command of any given situation. But how could he gain the advantage when he was the only one in the room who knew nothing about racehorses. Back in Charboneau's office, this assignment had sounded like a piece of cake. Waltz in, find the outlaws, bust them, go home.

But Michele Mallory had changed all that.

This incredible woman was in control here, not he. Who would have suspected such a feminine female to be so tough? And so full of knowledge? It wasn't often someone took Nick down a peg or two, but without even knowing it, Michele had done just that. For once, he wasn't the most authoritative person in the room. Never in all his thirty-four years had he met his match.

Until now.

There, sitting across from him, her soft red-gold hair floating against her chin, was the woman who could bring him to his knees. Her navy-blue eyes shone more gloriously than the midnight sky, her cinnamon scent more intoxicating than the most expensive whiskey, the taste of her lips more addicting than the sweetest nectar.

Nick stifled a groan. He couldn't stop fantasizing about her. To think a woman wielded such power over him, and yet, was so blithely unaware of her omnipotence.

Since the day he turned fifteen and tossed his derelict father out of the house, he'd been in control of not only his own destiny but his family's as well. He'd taken a job sacking groceries after school and on the weekends to help supplement his mother's income. And although his father's absence meant his mother had to work sixteen-hour shifts, she'd blossomed. Transforming herself from a battered wife with poor self-esteem into a cheerful, energetic businesswoman.

His mother's courage had inspired Nick to make something of himself. Even with the strain of family responsibilities, he'd maintained a 4.0 grade point average and graduated valedictorian with an academic scholarship to Texas A&M.

He'd known immediately that he wanted to be a policeman. To be on the front lines in the war against domestic violence, protecting women like his mother from tyrants like his father.

He'd worked and studied, throwing himself into his career with unbridled abandon. Was it any wonder his first wife, sweet little Julianna, had been overwhelmed by him?

Nick swallowed the last bite of Michele's hamburger mixture. It was damned good, and that surprised him. She'd professed she couldn't cook, and after he'd tricked her into the kitchen, he would have bet money she was going to sabotage the food just to get even. He certainly would have if the roles had been reversed.

But she hadn't stooped to temperamental impulse. She'd done the mature thing, leaving him feeling like a fool. The woman had bested him. No doubt about it.

And Nick hated to be bested, even by the best. Stealing another kiss, he mused, might be the way to even the score.

One by one the cowboys finished their meal, rinsed their dishes in the sink, and loaded them into the dishwasher.

"Don't worry about cooking breakfast," Jim Hollis told Michele. "We'll make do with cereal and fruit. Come join us at the stables in the morning. Five a.m."

"We'll be there." Michele beamed, and Nick wished like hell she was smiling at him.

"Ready to go to our cottage, honey?" Nick asked, possessively taking her arm. He had to make this show of affection believable. After all, he and Michele were supposed to be newlyweds.

Her muscles tensed beneath his fingers, but she did not

draw away. Steve Bradshaw gave them a sly grin, and Elvira offered to finish kitchen duty for Michele.

"Yeah, you two lovebirds go on and make yourselves at home in the cottage," Jim Hollis said, shuffling a deck of cards and dealing with the cowboys gathered. "We got a full day tomorrow, and I need to show you the office setup."

"Right." Nick nodded, barely cognizant of Jim's words. His attention was entirely focused on Michele's soft, creamy skin. "Good night, folks," Nick said and guided Michele toward the back door, his heart thumping like a snare drum.

"Night," several cowboys called in response.

Nick and Michele stepped out onto the back porch. The sun crawled down the horizon in a vivid blush of purple, pink, and orange. A scissortail called from a cottonwood tree. The aroma of roses hung in the air, mixing with Michele's cinnamon scent and stirring in Nick a strange sense of peace.

They walked up the road. Nick cast a wary glance back at the house. They couldn't afford slipups. Jim had been suspicious enough this afternoon when his lack of horse sense had quickly become apparent.

Tomorrow, when Hollis showed him the office, perhaps he could regain credibility. Tonight, he'd pump Michele for answers, cramming his head full of horse facts the way he'd crammed for algebra exams in college.

For appearances, Nick linked his arm through Michele's. She shot him an unreadable look.

What was she thinking? Was she nervous about spending the night alone with him in the cabin?

"I want to thank you," he said.

"For what?"

"For not spiking the food. I had no idea you could cook like that, and I fully expected you to dredge up some slop simply to get even with me."

"I...um...well..." she stammered. "Thank you."

"I'm offering to cook lunch tomorrow."

"Why?"

"I've got a confession," he admitted.

"What have you done, Nick?"

"Hollis never told me the hands didn't want you as manager. I made that up."

"What?"

"Now before you get all excited, let me explain. I hate to admit this, Mish, but I really do need you. If this investigation is going to work, we've got to act as a team."

"Well, well, well, the bigger they are, the harder they fall. About time you faced facts."

Nick stopped on the path outside the cottage and leaned close.

Michele drew back, folding her arms over her chest. Her lips were so kissably near, Nick had to swallow hard to keep from claiming her charming mouth. Her eyes widened in surprise as if she knew exactly what was on his mind.

"Nick," she warned in a whisper.

Nick.

The sound of his name dropped from her tongue like money from a slot machine. Wicked. It was plain wicked what she did to him without even trying. And to think they were going to have to sleep together, alone, in this small house.

"Let's get one thing straight, Nick. This pretend marriage is a charade for the cowboys. Once behind that closed door." She nodded at the house ". "You touch me, and there's going to be hell to pay."

"Michele Prescott," he answered. "I promise I won't touch you until you beg me to."

❄ 9 ❄

"Ha! Go ahead and hold your breath." Michele dashed into the cottage, desperately trying to wrangle the lusty emotions swelling in her chest.

Nick sauntered in behind her and plopped down onto the couch.

She busied herself unpacking her suitcases, then returned to the living room only when she felt able to control her feelings.

Nick was trying his best to wrestle out of his cowboy boots.

Michele watched, amused. He'd managed to work one foot halfway up the boot, but it had gotten stuck there. Kicking his leg in an attempt to extricate himself, he scowled at her.

"How do you remove these instruments of torture?"

"Bootjack."

His face brightened. "You got one?"

"No."

"Uh, could you please help me?" He flashed her that winsome "naughty boy" smile.

"Oh, for Pete's sake." Michele sighed. The last thing she wanted was to get close to Nickerson. She walked over and turned her back to him. "Put your foot between my legs."

"What did you say?" His sexy tone implied volumes.

"I'm not repeating myself, Nick. Do you want them off, or don't you?"

His boot made an instant appearance between her knees. Grasping the heel with the palm of one hand and slapping the other hand over the vamp of his foot, Michele tugged forward.

The boot resisted.

Great. Michele jerked again and almost pulled Nickerson off the couch.

"Whoa there, Nelly," he said, grasping the back of the furniture.

"This is it, Nick. If the boot doesn't come off this time, you're sleeping in them."

❦

MICHELE MALLORY HAD THE MOST DELICIOUS FANNY HE'D ever had the good fortune to peruse. Firm and round. Not too narrow, not too wide. All dressed up in tight blue jeans and wriggling oh so sweetly as she tried to rip the boot from his foot. Talk about compromising positions. What he wouldn't give to fill his hands with that soft tush and squeeze gently.

Sudden sweat beaded his brow.

"Awfully hot in here, isn't it?" He patted his forehead dry with his sleeve.

"Uh," Michele grunted, giving one last tug and tumbling across the room as the boot came free. Triumphantly, she held it aloft.

"One down, one to go." Nick wiggled his other foot.

To Nick's disappointment, the second boot came off much easier than the first, and in a matter of seconds, Michele had neatly arranged the boots side by side on the welcome mat.

"Want something to drink?" he asked.

Her hair was mussed from bending over, her oval face slightly flushed. She caught her bottom lip between her teeth, and that unconsciously provocative gesture had Nick spinning on his heels, headed for the kitchen in his socks.

"Fridge is bare," she reminded him. "We'll have to go to Rascal to stock up."

"How about a glass of cool water?" he called over his shoulder.

"Sounds great."

Filling two glasses with ice and tap water, Nick made his way back to the living room. He handed a glass to Michele, then set his own down on the coffee table. Immediately, she moved to manufacture a coaster from a piece of folded notepaper and slipped it under his drink.

Nick sprawled out on the couch and wedged an orange sofa pillow beneath his head. Retrieving the yellow notepad from the table where Michele had left it, he extracted a pen from his pocket. "Have a seat, Michele," he invited, clicking the pen.

Michele sat cross-legged on the floor in front of the coffee table, just inches away. If Nick leaned forward ever so slightly, his knuckles would brush her cheek.

"Okay," he said, "let's review what we know so far."

"For my money, the number one suspect is Steve Bradshaw."

"I agree the man is rather unsavory, but let's not jump to conclusions based on outward appearances."

"Elvira said Bradshaw was involved in some scheme with the previous owner, Lance Kane."

Nick doodled on the pad. "What kind of scheme?"

"When I tried to find out, Elvira clammed up," Michele said.

"You didn't press her?"

Michele furrowed her brow. "I didn't want to seem obvious, for heaven's sake."

"What about Elvira?"

"What about her?"

"She befriended you awfully quickly."

"So?"

"Could it be possible that she had an ulterior motive for getting so chummy?"

"She did."

Nick arched an eyebrow. "Yes."

"Elvira thought you were such a hunk that she came to find out just how stable our marriage is."

Nick grinned. "Did she now?"

"Yes. Don't ask me why, but she's under the impression you're the greatest thing since sliced bread."

"I am."

"Oh, please. I just ate supper. Don't make me throw up."

"So what did you tell her?"

Their gazes locked, held.

"About what?"

"Our marriage." How odd it sounded to say those words, but how sweet.

Michele snorted. "What choice did I have? I let her think we're wildly in love."

"Maybe you shouldn't have talked it up so much," Nick said. "She is kind of cute. And if I kissed her in all the right places, I bet she'd happily spill the beans about Bradshaw and Kane."

"You're not serious! You wouldn't actually jeopardize the investigation by coming on to her, would you?"

"What's the matter, Mish? Jealous?"

"Of you? Don't be ridiculous!" But a telltale spot of color belied her words.

"I'm just teasing, Mish. Can't you take a joke?"

"That wasn't funny."

"Anybody ever tell you that you have the sense of humor of a prune?"

Her mouth turned down at the corners, and she averted her eyes. He had only been trying to keep things light between them. He'd never meant to hurt her feelings. Shoot, Elvira couldn't hold a candle to the likes of Michele, but darn it, Michele was a serious woman, in desperate need of some levity in her life.

Clearing his throat, Nick looked down at the notepad in his hands. To his dismay, he'd written Michele's name ten times in rapid succession. Rattled at the way his subconscious mind had been traveling, Nick ripped out the page, wadded it up, and tossed it to the floor.

"Nick, you're a slob," she announced, getting to her feet and scooping up the paper.

Don't let her unfold it, Nick prayed.

"You remind me of that kid in the *Peanuts* comic strip." Michele shook her head. "You know, the messy one. Dirt trails him everywhere."

"Pigpen," Nick said, ripping another sheet of notepaper from the pad and chucking it on the floor, anything to distract her from reading what he'd written. "And I'm not a slob. You're a clean freak."

"Don't be ridiculous."

"Me? Ridiculous. We haven't even been here—" He consulted his watch. "Twenty minutes and already you've perfectly aligned my boots, put a coaster under my glass, and scolded me about paper on the floor." He ripped out another sheet and another, balling them up and hurling them around the room until the notepad was empty.

"You're driving me crazy," she muttered, snatching up the litter and stuffing it in a plastic bag.

"Can't you stop cleaning for one second?" he groused. "Chill out, babe."

"Don't call me 'babe,'" she growled through clenched teeth. "I just don't happen to like clutter."

"There's nothing wrong with clutter," he argued. "I'd say you were the one with the disorder. Obsessive-compulsive."

"Thanks for the diagnosis, Dr. Nick Freud."

"You're quite welcome, She-who-cleans-too-much."

"Does your mother know you're the world's biggest slob?" Michele asked, picking up the last of the paper.

"Are you kidding? Where do you think I learned to relax in clutter? Mom worked sixteen-hour shifts to support us throughout most of my childhood. When she had a day off, she said she wanted to spend her free time with her boys, not cleaning a house. To me, clothes on the floor, newspapers on the back of the couch, and laundry trailing out of the hamper are true signs of love."

☙❧

MICHELE STARED AT HIM, HER HAND COCKED AT HER HIP. Nick's revelation surprised her. During the three weeks that they'd been on stakeout last December, he'd been as close-mouthed about his family as she had about hers.

She wanted to know much more about this complex man, but the only way to get to know him better was to share a story in return, and Michele didn't know if she was ready for that.

"I suppose I'm excessively neat because of my childhood as well," she confessed at last.

"Oh?"

"My parents are both pretty demanding people. I felt I had to have some control over my own life and keeping things tidy was my way of achieving independence."

"Aha."

"What?" she asked, slightly irritated by his wide grin. Did she have something on her face? Had her lipstick smeared? Why was he staring at her like that?

"You're cute when you tell personal secrets," he said, swinging his legs to the floor and sitting upright.

Michele bit back a smart retort. She had to work with this infuriating man, and ruffling his feathers wouldn't solve the case. Besides, she'd come to the conclusion he liked sparring with her. When she didn't respond to his goading, she circumvented a showdown.

Not that she minded a confrontation. She enjoyed testing her mettle against a worthy opponent, but it was merely counterproductive in this situation, and the sooner they solved the case, the sooner she could get away from Nickerson.

"Let's stick to the subject at hand."

"Hey," he said, getting to his feet and crossing the room to place a hand on her shoulder. "I never meant to make you mad. Seems like we keep butting heads."

A shattering jolt of awareness skittered down her spine. Helpless to control her body's involuntary response to the man, she sucked in air. She was so conscious of his firm hand massaging her skin and his heady, masculine scent invading her nostrils that his very nearness raised the fine hairs on the back of her neck.

Heaven help her, she'd barely managed to escape his effects after the Harbarger case. That kiss he'd given her, well, she'd thought about it for weeks. Even after repeatedly telling herself it meant absolutely nothing, she could not stop thinking about him. Months had gone by, and she'd believed herself over that momentary infatuation.

Then...*bam*! Lieutenant Charboneau had dropped her right back into the lion's den.

"Michele," he whispered gruffly, his fingers tangling into her hair. "I'm sorry if I offended you. That was never my intent. I only wanted to lighten things between us."

"You didn't offend me," she said, holding her shoulders stiffly.

"No?"

"Not at all."

"Then why are your neck muscles as tight as guitar strings?" His fingers moved in circles to rub her tense muscles.

Michele edged away from him. "I think it's a good idea if we maintain a professional distance, don't you?"

"Ah, but we have to keep up the appearance of a happily married couple."

"Not when we're alone." She walked to the other side of the room and plunked down in an old wooden chair.

"Practice makes perfect."

"Cut the bull, Nick."

She had to regain control of this situation. Since they'd left the bunkhouse and Michele had allowed him to believe she'd cooked the evening meal, she'd felt like a fraud. But when he'd told her he admired her for not spiking the food, she'd enjoyed his compliment. And that had scared her more than anything. She'd been willing to sublimate her personality for his approval.

"You're a beautiful woman, Michele."

She stared down at her hands, terrified to meet his stare. "Knock off the baloney, Nick."

"I'm serious. Hasn't anyone ever sweet-talked you before?"

"Nope. I don't put up with false flattery."

"It's not false, Mish. I mean what I say."

Michele gulped. His compliments had softened her brains. She needed to get away from him and regroup.

"I'm going outside for some fresh air." She jumped to her feet and dashed out the door, her heart racing like a Thoroughbred on the last furlong.

The screen door snapped shut behind her. Michele strode across the porch in the warm summer twilight and listened to the night sounds—horses gently neighing, crickets chirping, bullfrogs croaking near the stock pond.

Okay, Michele, calm down. Take control. You must not let your heart rule your head.

She coached herself with the same words her father had used when he disciplined her for irrational behavior.

Judge Mallory demanded perfection, punishing her with his displeasure when she fell short of his expectations. And her mother had been no better, her requirements revolving around horses. Don't give that stallion so much rein, Michele Lauren. Lean forward, higher in the saddle. Use your crop. Let him know exactly who's boss.

Michele had ended up as the dupe in her parents' push-pull of wills. That was another reason Nickerson frightened her. Their constant clashing reminded her far too much of her parents' quixotic relationship.

She heard the door click shut. Nick's footsteps echoed behind her.

The scent of roses hung on the breeze. She stared up at the stars, waiting for him to speak, her pulse beating a rapid rhythm.

"Michele?"

Steeling herself, she inhaled deeply and turned to face her destiny.

Nick's face was hidden in the shadows, giving him the

spooky appearance of an unsavory outlaw. Not for the first time, she thought he could have easily ended up on the wrong side of the law. That silvery scar slashing starkly down his jaw proclaimed as much.

Michele gulped, grateful for the porch swing separating them. Pressure built inside her, taut and unpredictable. He'd tugged his boots back on, she noticed, and his hair hung in shaggy disarray.

"Michele," he said, "I'm sorry if I insulted you."

"You didn't." She shrugged. Never admit a weakness. That was her motto.

"Elvira's a nice girl, but she can't hold a candle to you."

"Elvira? What are you talking about?"

"That remark I made earlier."

"You think I'm jealous?" Michele splayed a palm across her chest.

"Yes. But you shouldn't be..."

"Of all the egotistical, bigheaded, cockamamy things I've ever heard. You think I'm *jealous* over you, Nick?" Michele threw back her head and barked out a laugh, but inside, her stomach squeezed tight.

"You did get your nose out of joint when I made a joke about kissing her."

"That's absolutely ridiculous." She raised her chin and met his gaze with a defiant stare. Not for a minute would she dare let on that he'd hit so close to the truth that her knees trembled.

"Is it?" His voice rumbled rich and deep in his chest. Nick moved toward her, skirting the porch swing and setting it in motion as he walked by.

The chain's creaking coincided with the roaring of her heart. Michele tried to stand her ground, but he kept coming closer.

"That's far enough," she said, her voice as shaky as her

legs. She didn't even want to consider what might happen if he touched her again.

"What are you so afraid of, Michele?" he asked, his voice low. "Who hurt you?"

"Nobody." She clenched her jaw, steeling herself.

That was true. She had never let anyone get close enough. Michele preferred to live life on the edge, in a highly amplified, fully energized state. Like now, the voice in the back of her head nudged. That sort of existence didn't bode well for marriage and children. She wanted to stay single, and the only way to do that was to keep her heart unfettered, her mind fully alert at the helm.

"Relax. I'm not trying to knock a hole in your armor."

But he already had! Just staring into his hypnotic eyes, she felt all her strength drain away.

"I don't want an entanglement any more than you do."

"That's good." Damn. Why did her voice quiver?

"But, glory, woman, you do stir me physically and challenge me mentally. Do you have any idea how rare that is?"

Did she ever. He did the very same thing to her. Never had a man created such commotion inside her.

"We're both dedicated professionals. We can't afford to jeopardize our careers or this case for a passing affair," she said firmly.

"I agree completely," Nick said. "But it is a shame. I have a feeling that you and I could really steam the sheets."

🏵 10 🏵

What an understatement.

If he ever coaxed Michele into his bed, Nick had a strong feeling the sheets would melt clean through the bed frame. She was right. They couldn't risk a fling, but what he wouldn't give to wrap his body around hers for one long, endless night.

The kiss he'd given her that afternoon hung in his mind, a heady promise of what could be. He yearned for another taste of her sweet lips, to bury his face in that fluff of blond hair. Even thinking about it aroused him. He gulped past the boulder blocking his throat.

He took another step closer.

Michele stood her ground, but he could tell from the wide-eyed expression on her delicate, oval face that she longed to run.

Cautiously, he reached out and cupped her cheek with his palm. The moonlight glinted off her face, giving her the appearance of an alabaster statue—perfect and pristine.

God, how he wanted her! More than he'd ever wanted

anyone, and the intensity of that desire rocked Nick to his very soul.

They were too much alike for anything to come of this hungry craving. Even if they weren't on an undercover assignment together, a relationship between the two of them was out of the question. They both placed their careers first and foremost. Any lover would trail a pale second to law enforcement.

Stroking her chin with his thumb, Nick heard her choke back a strangled moan. He lowered his head to kiss her.

Michele wrapped a hand around his wrist and stared up at him. "No," she whispered.

"Ah, Mish," his voice cracked.

He recognized her longing to pull away, to flee. He could see doubt reflected in the depths of her navy-blue eyes, but sheer bravery overrode her fear, and she stayed grafted to the spot.

He knew the feeling. The need to run conflicting with the need to prove oneself. In a flash, his memory transported him back to that squalid apartment in South Houston where his father had beaten his mother for the last time.

For once, Nick had not escaped to the bedroom he shared with his three younger brothers. Instead, he'd placed himself between his mother and his sorry excuse for a father, thrust out his jaw, and challenged the old man to a fight.

He'd been terrified, his legs liquid jelly, but he'd stood up to the tyrant, and Nick had exulted at his eventual triumph. From that night on, he'd never run from another fight.

Somewhere along the way, Michele had experienced the same lofty taste of power. Somewhere, she'd learned to fight for what she believed in. Somewhere, this magnificent woman had discovered how to stand up to injustice. Courage was a potent aphrodisiac, and Michele Mallory possessed it in spades.

They were polar twins, he and Michele. Their moral and ethical values the same. They were both bold, aggressive, authoritative. But where he was reckless, she was circumspect. He was a slob and she a neat freak. He was fire, and she was hot ice. He was night and she was day. So much alike, yet such opposites.

Opposites attract. The words leaped to his mind.

Kissing her would hurt nothing. They were, after all, supposed to be newlyweds.

Nick stared down at Michele and cupped her chin in his hand. He saw the same raw desire reflected in her eyes.

Their gazes connected with the fervor of a lightning bolt striking a hundred-year-old oak tree, demolishing all willpower, all prudence. Nothing mattered but this moment and their desperate aching need.

"Nick..." she said, but never finished the sentence.

With a rattle of indrawn breath, Nick dipped his head and took possession of her mouth. Fiercely, like a warrior vanquishing an enemy, he claimed her as his own.

And as he hoped she would, Michele met his challenge. Rising on tiptoes to return the crashing vigor of his kiss, she attacked his lips with a hunger that had his heart slamming against his chest.

Glory, how he admired her! Her strength, her passion, her lust for life.

Her skin rippled like raw silk beneath his touch, her lithe body more receptive than an exotic flower opening its blooms to the sun. She sighed into his mouth, sharp and poignant, her basic sounds throwing kerosene on the inferno raging within him.

Tangling her fingers in his hair, she tugged his head lower.

The quiet evening was in direct contrast to the tempest seething inside them. The wind was still; their passion was not. Her hands roamed his back, communicating the restless energy anxious to be freed.

Nick groaned. He knew their joining would be incredible, like no sexual experience he'd ever known. In Michele Mallory, he had at long last met his match.

Her tongue darted out, coaxing him, teasing him beyond endurance.

He wanted to scoop her into his arms, and like Rhett Butler sweeping Scarlet up the staircase, carry her into the bedroom and bury his body in hers with a force that could destroy them both.

No.

He would not lose control. Would not jeopardize the investigation, not even for the sumptuous gift waiting in front of him.

Nick broke away, chanting, "Michele, Michele, Michele." The burning in his groin was unbelievable. His chest rose and fell with a heavy rhythm as he held her at arm's length.

Passion glazed her eyes as she clung to him, trembling with the force of their kiss.

Like a dreamer waking from a trance, Michele shook her head and ran a finger across her swollen lips.

"Um." She breathed softly.

Through the open screen door, the harsh jangling of the telephone pierced the quiet. Nick placed a hand to his sweat-drenched brow.

"We better answer that," he said.

Michele nodded and stepped away from him, confusion on her face. He knew exactly how she felt.

Turning his back on her, Nick wrenched the door open and stalked into the cottage as the phone shrilled for the third time. He heard Michele's footsteps behind him as he answered it.

"Hello," he rasped.

"Nick? Hollis here. Get over to the stables. We've got a big problem."

"What's wrong?" Nick asked, but Hollis had already hung up.

⚜

ON THE SHORT RIDE TO THE STABLES, MICHELE COULDN'T stop thinking about that damned kiss. Although kiss was an understatement. More like a nuclear meltdown. The magnetic bonding of Nick's lips to her defied description.

In the quiet of the pickup truck, Michele listened to his ragged breathing. The gruff sound sent spikes of desire tripping down her spine. What would have happened between them if the phone had not rung?

Michele did not want to think about that.

Floodlamps threw bright light across the area. Ranch hands ringed the holding paddock, their faces drawn and serious. Elvira stood to one side, an ice pack pressed to her temple, Jim Hollis's reassuring hand clamped on her shoulder.

"Something's happened to one of the horses," Michele exclaimed and leaped from the truck before Nick braked to a complete stop.

She hit the ground running, fear spurting adrenaline through her veins.

Inside the paddock the lively iron-gray Thoroughbred she'd noticed earlier that day was galloping around the ring, his eyes rolling wildly, froth spewing from his lips, empty saddle stirrups bouncing against his flanks. The young gelding repeatedly tossed his head. His breathing was labored, his body covered in sweat.

Something was very wrong. The animal was spirited, yes, but this bizarre manifestation went far beyond nature.

One of the stable hands twirled a rope, but every time the

cowboy approached within throwing distance, the horse would rear up and paw the air like a crazed thing, sending the cowboy scrambling for safety.

"What happened?" Michele demanded, joining Jim and Elvira.

"Whirlwind went plumb crazy, Michele," Elvira said. "After supper, I went out to the stables. He was so restless I thought I'd bring him out to the track and breeze him. But the minute I got on, he lost his head." Elvira gulped in air. Her petite body trembled.

"It's okay. Take a deep breath."

The jockey took a deep breath, then let it out through clenched teeth. "I managed to wrangle him into the paddock, but then he threw me." She lowered the ice pack, giving Michele a good view of the wicked purple knot swelling at her temple.

Michele winced and turned her attention back to the iron-gray who showed no sign of calming. His heart rate must be dangerously high, and if something wasn't done soon, the horse might die.

"How long has this been going on?" she asked.

"About fifteen minutes. We've called Dr. Felix," Jim said.

Michele rubbed her brow and prayed the vet would hurry. The iron-gray looked near exhaustion, but he kept relentlessly circling the paddock. Had the horse been drugged? It certainly looked as if that was the case.

Could Elvira be involved? Michele cast a glance at the tormented jockey. She didn't want to believe it. Who else might dope the horse and why? The young gelding was still too immature to present a challenge on the racetrack.

Nick pressed a palm to the small of Michele's back and inclined his head, indicating he wanted to speak with her in private. The pressure of his hand against her spine resurrected the feelings she'd pushed aside. Quickly, she stepped away.

"What's going on?" he whispered when they were out of earshot of the others.

"It looks like Whirlwind might have been drugged."

"Who did it?"

She shrugged. "I don't know."

His dark eyes glistened. Michele saw frustration in the tense set of his shoulders and jaw. Nickerson was accustomed to being in charge, and now he had to rely on her expertise. Before he could ask any more questions, Dr. Felix drove into the yard.

"At last," Michele mumbled, relieved both to see the doctor and distance herself from Nickerson.

Dr. Felix rushed toward the paddock, medical bag in his hand.

Chattering at once, Jim and Elvira filled him in on what had happened.

"I'll give Whirlwind a sedative," Dr. Felix said, rummaging around in his black bag. "But someone's got to catch him so I can get close enough."

"Everyone get a rope," Jim Hollis directed. "This a group effort."

Dr. Felix withdrew a vial from his bag and filled a plastic syringe.

The ranch hands grabbed ropes. Jim Hollis stood at the gate, shouting instructions. Michele readjusted her ponytail. This wasn't going to be easy.

NICK HUNG BACK WITH ELVIRA, WATCHING AS MICHELE and the cowhands cautiously entered the paddock.

He felt utterly useless, and Nick hated being in a subordinate position. He should be the one to rope the gelding, to fight the unruly beast. But he lacked the appropriate skills and knowledge.

For the first time in many years, Nick came face-to-face with his own personal limitations. He wanted to solve the problem, take charge, handle everything. He should be helping Michele, not standing idly by.

Frustrated, Nick gritted his teeth. Where had he developed this obsessive need to control every situation? How was he supposed to deal with it? Why did he feel threatened by Michele?

Simple, you fool, a voice in the back of his mind insisted, you want to impress her.

Brushing back that thought, Nick clung to the paddock gate, his heart thudding curiously slow as his gaze focused on Michele.

She and the five cowhands twirled their ropes in unison.

The gelding ran right, stopped, then darted left.

Six ropes fell at once. Three successfully snagged the animal around the neck. One of the three ropes belonged to Michele. She gave a triumphant whoop.

The horse let out a keening scream and jerked his head, his nostrils flaring in anger. Michele and the cowhands dug in their heels.

Nick couldn't take his eyes off her. She was magnificent, hanging tough, battling the gelding like her life depended on it. Her gloved hands were twisted around the rope, her arm muscles bunched with effort, her hair streaming out behind her like a moon goddess.

He had never seen anything so beautiful. Michele Mallory was an intriguing paradox. Dainty, yet tough. Kind, yet firm. Sweet, yet oh so tart.

God above, how he wanted this woman!

The burning in his heart, in his groin, in his very soul,

shocked Nick. He was too single-minded for such an intense relationship. He loved control too much to give himself over to this heady, inefficient emotion. He could lose himself in a union with Michele Mallory, and Nick had fought his entire life for a strong, separate identity. He would not willingly sacrifice his independence.

They tussled with Whirlwind, Jim Hollis jumping into the fray until the agitated gelding had been subdued enough to allow Dr. Felix to approach.

What potion had the good doctor concocted? Could the vet be behind the doping?

Eagle-eyed, Nick watched as Dr. Felix injected the horse.

"Aren't you going to draw blood from Whirlwind?" Michele asked.

"Uh, what for?" Felix looked uncomfortable.

"To see why he's acting this way."

"Well, yeah, sure." Extracting a red-topped tube from his jacket pocket, Dr. Felix drew blood from the frightened animal's vein, then stuck the tube in his black bag and stepped away from the horse.

"Keep holding him until he calms," Felix instructed.

While the rest of the cowboys were engaged with the iron-gray, Michele broke away from the group and walked over to where Nick and Dr. Felix were standing outside the paddock gate.

"What's your diagnosis, Doctor?" Michele asked.

Dr. Felix shook his head. "I have no idea. Very spooky."

"Could Whirlwind have been drugged?" Nick asked, not one to pussyfoot around a subject. Taking full advantage of the fact they were playing newlyweds, Nick draped his arm across Michele's shoulders.

"For what earthly reason?" The vet frowned.

"You tell me."

"I suppose someone could be trying to disqualify him for

this weekend's race. But do you seriously suspect someone here at Triple Fork would do such a thing? These folks love their horses."

Nick shrugged. "People will do strange things when money is involved."

"Actually, Mr. Prescott," Dr. Felix said, his tone frosty, "you and your wife are the newcomers here. Perhaps we should be asking you the tough questions."

"Touché," Nick said, his smile deadly.

"Why don't we wait to draw conclusions until the blood has been tested?" Felix patted his black bag.

"You'll call us as soon as you know something," Nick stated.

"But of course." Felix forced a smile.

"Appreciate it."

"Call me if anything else goes wrong," Felix said.

The vet gave Hollis detailed instructions on Whirlwind's care, then got in his pickup and drove away.

Michele took Nick's arm and dragged him over to one side. "We need to get that blood sample," she hissed. "Tonight. In case Felix is involved, we don't want to give him the opportunity to tamper with the specimen."

"What's the point? Charboneau says the drugs can't be detected by laboratory tests."

"Bingo. If the test is negative, it's an encouraging sign we're onto the illegal doping operation. I swear to you, Nick, Whirlwind is under the influence of chemicals. Did you notice Felix readily agreed to the testing? If he's involved, he thinks he's got nothing to hide. We've got to get our hands on that specimen."

"Ah," Nick said, rubbing his hands together. "A little B and E. Right up my alley."

"You're incorrigible," she whispered.

"And you love that about me, don't you?"

"I do not," Michele said, but she grinned.

Nick's heart stammered at the sight of her turned-up lips. Ah, hell, it was awfully disconcerting to realize what the woman could do to him with a mere smile.

"Let's get at it, then. You round things up with Hollis. I'll go back to the cottage, alert Charboneau, and pick up my bag of tricks."

"Your what?"

"Hide and watch, Mrs. Prescott." He winked.

Michele turned and headed back to the paddock. Nick watched her back pockets swaying like palm trees in a tropical paradise. The pressure against the zipper of his blue jeans grew with each swish of her glorious fanny.

One way or the other, something had to give.

And soon.

11

"Shhh," Nick raised a finger to his lips. He shined a flashlight at the back door of Dr. Felix's clinic on the outskirts of Rascal. They'd followed the vet from the Triple Fork, keeping a safe distance behind him.

Nick had called Charboneau from the cottage and arranged for a courier to meet them in Marfa as soon as possible to pick up the blood sample and whisk it off to Austin for analysis.

"I didn't say anything," Michele protested, her pulse ticking along like a stopwatch.

"No, but you're breathing loud enough to wake the dead."

"Well, excuse me for living," Michele whispered harshly. "But I've never committed a crime before." She made a conscious effort to slow her breathing.

Nick shined the flashlight under his chin, giving him the appearance of a wicked jack-o'-lantern, and peered over his shoulder at her. "Never?"

"Well, maybe I exceeded the speed limit a few times, but that's it."

"May I remind you, Miss Holier-than-Thou, that it was your idea to retrieve the blood sample tonight."

"I take it you *have* committed a crime?"

"Yes. I did become familiar with the inside of a station house in the days of my misspent youth."

"Ha! I knew you were a juvenile delinquent. Bet you had a Harley and wore chains."

He gave her a dangerous look. "Better watch out for me, babe, I'm a bad boy."

Michele suppressed a shiver. She wasn't afraid of Nickerson. Was she?

"This is too easy," he said, playing the flashlight beam along the windows and doors. "Doc Felix doesn't even have an alarm system."

"The benefits of small-town living."

"You'd think if he were involved in the doping, he'd be more careful."

"Maybe he's so cocky, he's careless."

"In my old neighborhood, this place would have been stripped bare in two hours," Nick mused.

"How in the world did you end up on the right side of the law?" Michele asked.

"Long story."

"You'll have to tell me about it sometime."

"Boring stuff, Mish. Any psychologist can spout a thousand case histories just like mine."

A tug of empathy pulled at her chest. What exactly had Nickerson's childhood been like? What demons had he overcome to achieve his current role in society as defender and protector?

Nick hunkered down on his knees and opened a black shaving kit he carried under his arm. Instead of shaving cream and razors, however, the bag contained burglary tools.

Michele shook her head. "I don't believe this."

"Tools of the undercover trade. Get used to it."

"What do you mean by that?" she asked.

"You're an undercover cop now. Forget uniform. Here, hold the flashlight."

"But I don't want to leave uniform duty," she protested, leaning over to shine the light on the lock.

"You won't have a choice."

"Excuse me?"

"After my recommendation."

Michele stood perfectly still. "What recommendation?"

"That you be promoted." The lock clicked, and the door sprung open. Nick got to his feet, bowed, and swept his hand for her to enter. "Ta-da."

Nickerson was recommending her for a promotion? That must mean he thought well of her work. The notion that she'd impressed Nick had her stomach in knots. Despite their arguments, or maybe because of them, she admired him. And he respected her.

Even after she'd turned him in to Internal Affairs for his behavior in the Harbarger fiasco.

And then another, darker thought occurred to her. Perhaps this was just Nickerson's cunning ploy to get her into bed.

"I appreciate the offer," she said, stepping over the threshold into the veterinarian's office. "But no, thanks."

"Are you serious?"

"I don't want to be beholden to you for any favors."

His hand reached out to squeeze her arm. "What's that supposed to mean?"

"I'm not trading sexual favors for a promotion recommendation."

"Well, who the hell asked you?" he snapped, releasing her arm and moving through the office, the flashlight beam cutting a swath through the blackness.

Immediately contrite for jumping to conclusions, Michele ducked her head.

"What are we looking for, anyway?" Nick asked harshly.

"A refrigerator."

"Over there." The light glinted against a large, white, oblong box, sitting in one corner.

She followed him across the room. They reached the refrigerator only to find another lock in place.

"Where's my bag?" he asked.

"By the back door."

"Could you go get it, please?" His tone was frosty.

Michele turned and was inching her way back toward the door when she heard the low, menacing growl.

※

MICHELE TOOK ANOTHER STEP, AND THE GROWL DEEPENED.

"Nick," she whispered. Michele had been terrified of dogs since a neighbor's Chihuahua had bitten her ankles when she was a child.

"What is it?"

"I think I found out why Dr. Felix doesn't have an alarm system." Her voice quavered.

At that moment, the growls dissolved into ferocious barking. White fangs glittered in the cloak of shadows less than six feet from Michele's foot.

The dog was huge, black, and wearing a leather collar studded with spikes. He was one of those ferocious guard dogs, a Doberman or Rottweiler, Michele couldn't remember which.

"Don't move!" Nick commanded.

He need not have worried. She was welded to the spot.

The dog's mouth curled back in an ugly snarl, the intensity of his bark almost deafening.

"Nick," Michele warbled. "I'm scared."

"Hang on, babe."

Babe. The word comforted. She heard Nick rustling around behind her. What was he doing?

The dog advanced, his jaws snapping obscenely. Michele struggled with her fear. She knew dogs could smell terror. She tried to take a deep breath, but her airway seemed constricted.

A loud crash sounded behind her, but she was too frightened to glance back. The sound, however, did command the dog's full attention.

"Here, Fido," Nick called.

Michele's heart slammed into her chest as she watched the dog crouch.

"Be careful," she urged.

"Come on, you ugly son of a—"

The dog sprang.

Ducking, Michele whipped her head around and saw Nick sprint through the office, the gruesome creature snapping at his heels.

Oh my gosh, he's going to be eaten alive!

"Hey!" Michele shouted, knocking over an office chair to draw the beast's attention her way.

The dog skidded to a stop, then swiveled his massive head from Nick to Michele and back again, slobber flying from his lips.

Her diversion bought Nick enough time to open the door connecting the office to the kennels. A chorus of howls assaulted their ears.

The dog looked confused.

"Hey, Fido," Nick said, fanning a floor mat in front of the door. "Nice poochy."

The dog lunged.

Michele bit back a scream.

In a flash, the beast sank his teeth into Nick's arm.

With the sure movements of a true warrior, Nick clamped the floor mat around the dog's head, pried him from his arm and bodily hurled the brute down the hallway toward the kennel. Before the stunned animal could charge again, Nick slammed and locked the door.

The dog let out an enraged howl and crashed its body against the wooden barrier.

"Let's get that damned blood sample and get out of here," Nick said. Bending, he picked up the flashlight which had gotten knocked to the floor in the fracas.

Michele wrapped her arms around her body to keep from trembling. She hadn't been this frightened since the night she'd been shot.

"You okay?" Nick placed a hand on her shoulder.

She nodded, perilously close to tears. Cops weren't supposed to cry.

The dog's angry noises echoed eerily throughout the darkened room.

Michele followed Nick like a sleepwalker. She felt cold all over. Standing next to him, she held the flashlight while he successfully picked the refrigerator lock. He wrenched open the door, and they peered in at the row of blood specimens.

"Damn," Nick swore under his breath. "Which one belongs to Whirlwind?"

"Take them all," Michele said. "We'll let Charboneau sort them out."

Nick stashed the blood tubes in his black bag, and they left the office, the sounds of the irate guard dog still ringing in their ears.

After rendezvousing with the courier, they drove back to the Triple Fork. By the time they trudged into the cottage, it was well past midnight.

Sighing, Michele flipped on the lights as they stepped inside. "What a day," she exclaimed, slumping onto the sofa.

"Yeah," Nick grunted. "And we've got to be up at five."

"Don't remind me," Michele groaned. She glanced up to meet his gaze, then gasped and jumped to her feet. "Nick," she cried. "You're bleeding."

Nick looked down at his torn sleeve. Dried blood caked the plaid material. He winced. "Fido took a little nip."

"For heaven's sake, sit down." She placed a hand to his chest and pushed him backward into a chair. "I've got a first aid kit in my pickup."

"It's no big deal," he protested. "Just a scratch."

"Stop playing macho cop. When was the last time you had a tetanus shot?"

"A year ago."

"That's good. Hang on, I'll be right back." Michele dashed outside to the truck, her pulse spurting through her veins with each step, her stomach coiling in empathy with Nick's wound.

He'd been protecting her when he'd gotten hurt, deflecting the dog's wrath onto himself. That knowledge jarred her.

Nick would have done the same for anyone, she told herself. He's that kind of guy.

So why did she feel this funny, fizzy sensation somewhere in the general region of her heart?

Retrieving the first aid kit, she hurried back into the cottage, trying her best to chase away such dangerous feelings.

Nick sat in the chair, his head thrown back, eyes closed, chest rising and falling in a smooth rhythm.

"Nick?" She called his name and placed a warm hand on his arm.

"Hmm?" he asked dreamily.

"Wake up; we've got to dress that wound."

"It's not so bad," he murmured, his eyelids fluttering. "Let me sleep."

"Your shirtsleeve is saturated with blood. Now get up and come to the bathroom."

Reluctantly, he opened one eye. "Slave driver."

"Come on, get up," she insisted.

She took his hand and tugged him to his feet. Grunting, Nick shuffled behind her into the bathroom.

"Sit." Michele shut the toilet lid, and Nick obeyed.

Opening the first aid kit, Michele became acutely aware of the close confines and Nick's distracting aura.

His masculine scent teased her nostrils, and the raw blisters on his palms strummed her heartstrings. He should have worn gloves today when helping Hollis with the horses. A part of her wanted to take his hands in hers and gently kiss each tender blister.

"Let's get you out of that shirt," she said.

"I thought you'd never ask." Despite his exhaustion, the grin he gave her was purely wicked.

"Knock off the sexual innuendos."

"But that's no fun."

"It's too late for fun."

"It's never too late for that kind of fun."

"Nick," she warned. "I've got rubbing alcohol in this bag, and I won't hesitate to pour it over your wound. Off with the shirt. Now."

"Mish, you're the bossiest damned female I ever met." A sultry expression flickered in his black eyes.

"Absolutely, Nick. Strip."

NICK RAISED HIS WOUNDED ARM TO UNBUTTON HIS SHIRT. Fresh pain shot through him. He grimaced.

"Here," she said. "Let me do it."

Usually, he would have resisted, shrugged off the pain. But there was something very pleasing about having Michele Mallory on her knees in front of him, her nimble fingers working to loosen his shirt buttons. He made the decision to lean back and enjoy.

Michele's blond head hovered just below his chin. It took every ounce of willpower he possessed not to wrap his arms around her, pull her to his chest, and kiss her just as passionately as he had earlier on the front porch. Could only a few hours have passed since then? The pressure building below his belt made it seem much longer.

"Slip your arm out," she said, once his shirt was unbuttoned.

Fighting hard to resist nature's urges, Nick struggled out of the shirt, sucking in his breath as he pulled the blood-encrusted material from his open wound.

"It looks sore," she said, leaning closer to peer at the bite mark.

"Why don't you kiss it and make it better."

Michele ignored his remark. "Some bruising, a little swelling. You'll live."

"That's nice to know."

She smelled wonderful, a dazzling combination of cinnamon and pure unadulterated woman. He had a sudden image of their naked bodies pressed together, writhing on the bathroom floor.

Briefly closing his eyes, Nick gulped past the passion clogging his throat. His body craved Michele like a cactus hungered for sunshine.

She untwisted the cap from a hydrogen peroxide bottle. Armed with cotton-tipped swabs, antibiotic ointment, and adhesive dressings, she busied herself with his wound. Wrappers rustled. Nick watched her dip the cotton swab sticks into the peroxide.

"This may sting."

He bit back a curse as she scrubbed the damaged area with damp cotton.

"That dog really chewed on you." Her breath warmed his skin; her fingers curled around his upper arm.

"Yeah," he said, his voice gruff with longing.

What in the hell was wrong with him? No woman had ever dominated his thoughts the way this one did. He was a professional on undercover assignment; he'd do well to remember that fact.

Her breasts grazed his bare chest as she leaned over him. The feel of her tender flesh and the soft sounds of her breathing had Nick fighting hard to restrain his response to her femininity.

"Does it hurt?"

"Not much."

"Maybe we should take you to a doctor."

"And tell them what?" Nick challenged. "That we were breaking into the vet's office? That would do wonders for our cover."

"I suppose you're right."

12

She looked up at him. His eyes glistened with unexpressed passion. Dropping her gaze, she squeezed antibiotic ointment onto a dry swab stick and dabbed at his arm.

Since squatting down in front of him, she'd done her best not to acknowledge the sensations coursing through her. But there was no way she could ignore his superb body. A band of muscles rippled across his chest. His biceps were as big around as her thighs. His complexion was tanned, the hair on his chest dark and curly.

What would it feel like to be crushed in his embrace? To run her tongue along his salty skin? To feel his body moving inside hers?

Forcing herself to concentrate on his wound, Michele focused her eyes on the four puncture marks, now cleansed free of blood, and struggled to shove all sexual thoughts from her mind. Unconsciously, she kneaded the ointment tube tighter in her fist until a big wad of the sticky stuff squirted over her hand in one plop.

"Darn it," she whispered, wiping the goo on a piece of toilet paper.

"What's wrong?" Nick asked.

"Nothing," she mumbled. Nothing, except that his nearness had turned her mind to mush.

Quickly, she finished her work, pasting an adhesive bandage over the bite marks. When she stood up, blood rushed from her head, leaving her dizzy and more than a little discombobulated. She had to do something, anything, to remove herself from these close quarters and Nick Nickerson's magnetic attractions.

"All done," she croaked, backing away from him.

"Thanks." He stood up.

"Well," she said. "Time for bed."

"Yes."

"I'll sleep on the couch," she offered. After all, he'd gotten bitten on her behalf.

"No," he said. "You take the bed."

"I insist. Please."

"We could share." He raised his uninjured arm. "I'll be good, I swear. We can sleep on top of the covers with our clothes on. Face it, Mish. That couch is about as comfortable as sleeping in a toolbox."

Did she dare?

"Don't worry about me, Nick; I've slept in worse places," she said glibly.

He stared at her for a long moment, then shook his head. "Suit yourself. But you're welcome to join me on the bed."

Turning on her heels, Michele ran from the bathroom before her libido got the best of her and she foolishly took him up on his offer.

NICK SANG AT THE TOP OF HIS LUNGS, SNATCHING MICHELE from the first good twenty minutes of sleep she'd had the entire night. The sound of running water accompanied his impromptu serenade.

Groaning, she turned over, curled her hands beneath her cheek, and tried unsuccessfully to go back to sleep. A sofa spring poked her in the ribs, the call of nature nudged her bladder, and her arms ached, stiff and sore from wrangling the hyperactive iron-gray the evening before.

"My-o-my, what a wonderful day."

Someone should shoot him, Michele thought rather uncharitably. No one had a right to be so cheerful at four-thirty in the morning, especially a man who 'd been bitten by a dog. Nickerson had the singing voice of a scalded cat.

Sighing, Michele tossed off the sheet and dragged herself to a sitting position. Her head felt stuffed with cotton, her mouth as dry as week-old doughnuts. She sank her face into her palms and tried to work up some enthusiasm for the day ahead.

Michele had finally collapsed on the sofa around one a.m., and even then, blessed rest had escaped her. For some inexplicable reason, no matter how hard she tried to calm her swirling mind, she couldn't stop thinking about Nickerson and the fact he lay just a few feet away with nothing separating them but a thin wooden door.

Despite her best efforts, the man had gotten into her blood. The very idea scared her to death. Having such fantasies about her colleague was unprofessional and could jeopardize the investigation. Yet, how did she go about resisting the age-old urge of physical desire?

It could never work out, she reminded herself. She and Nick were too much alike in some ways, too different in others.

She must put her rollercoaster emotions in the deep

freeze. Now. Before it was too late and she got hurt. Sharing a cottage, pretending to be married, made her task that much harder. Michele swore to fall back on her famous self-control, keep her features deadpan, her tongue sharp, and most of all, stay as far away from Nickerson as she could manage under the circumstances.

The bathroom door wrenched open, and a rectangle of light spilled into the hallway. Nick stepped through the door, a fluffy white towel wrapped around his narrow waist, his damp hair glistening darkly.

He stood silhouetted, the perfect specimen of manhood, from his broad muscular chest to his trim legs. Resisting his considerable charms was going to be a hard assignment indeed.

Michele tried her best not to stare at him, but it was hard. The strip of terry cloth covering the lower part of his anatomy was held together by his thumb and forefinger, and in spite of herself, she couldn't help wondering exactly what attributes that towel disguised.

"Good morning, my bride," Nick chirped, more chipper than a cheerleader on a chocolate high. How dare he be so perky.

He walked into the living room and turned on the over-head lamp.

"Shut up." Michele scowled, squinting against the light. She wished desperately that his mother had seen fit to drown him at birth.

"I take it you're not a morning person."

"It's not morning," she groused. "It's the middle of the night."

"I'll brew a pot of coffee while you shower. That'll make a world of difference," he predicted.

"Humph. There ought to be a law against perkiness before six a.m." Moving slowly, she roused herself from the couch.

"How did you sleep?" he asked, shaking his head.

Water droplets patterned her skin. "Lousy."

"You should have gotten into bed with me."

"Don't be ridiculous," she snapped, her body heating up at the very thought of lying next to this potent man.

"Afraid you couldn't keep your hands off me, eh?" He grinned.

Heavens yes. "Don't flatter yourself."

"I'll take the couch tonight," he promised.

"Good." She could barely look at him.

"Michele..." He moved closer.

"Yes?" Michele gulped. Her instincts screamed for her to get away.

"Never mind."

Something shifted in his eyes. What it was she couldn't tell. Rapidly, Michele propelled herself toward the safety of the bathroom. What had Nick been about to say?

That question plagued her as she showered, dressed, and pulled her hair back in a ponytail. By the time she reappeared in blue jeans and a purple knit T-shirt, Nick was sipping coffee and buttering toast.

He'd dressed in faded denim jeans that hung low on his narrow hips, clearly accentuating his considerable attributes. His black hair, still damp, curled down his neck, just inviting her fingers to curry through it. But most distracting of all, he still hadn't put on a shirt. There was something incredibly tantalizing about his bare chest.

"Feeling better?" he asked.

"Not particularly." She reached for the mug he offered and stirred in a sugar packet.

"Too bad."

"How's your arm?" she asked, to be polite.

He glanced at the bandaged wound on his left biceps. "Sore."

"I'm sorry about that."

"All part of the job," he murmured, blowing across his coffee.

Damn. Did she have to be so mesmerized by his pursed lips, those white teeth, that extraordinary washboard stomach?

She leaned against the counter and tried her best to stop staring at him. The harder she fought this attraction, the more difficult it was to deny him.

"I thought one of us might search Hollis's office today."

"Looking for what?" She concentrated on the buttered toast in her right hand.

Nick shrugged. "Whatever turns up. Maybe examine the records on Whirlwind. You know he was supposed to race at Manor Downs on Saturday."

"All right. Me or you?"

"Whoever gets the opportunity."

"I'll do it," Michele said, brushing breadcrumbs from her fingers and shooting him a smart-aleck glance. "After all, you're cooking lunch for the hands."

"Okay."

She expected an argument, and his easy acquiescence knocked her off-balance. She wanted to pick a fight with him, entice him to rise to the bait in hopes that getting angry would dampen these erotic thoughts her mind insisted upon concocting.

"You don't have to sound so agreeable," she snapped.

Nick looked at her, surprised. "You wanted an argument?"

Yes. No. Oh, hell, she didn't know what she wanted. She just wished Nickerson would cover his naked torso.

"We better get going," she said, taking one last swallow of

coffee before rinsing her cup in the sink. "We've got a long day ahead of us."

"You can say that again," he muttered.

"Don't start with me, Nick, I'm not in the mood."

"Michele, a cobra wouldn't be stupid enough to mess with you," he replied icily before stalking out of the room and leaving Michele to wonder just what in the heck she was trying to prove.

🐜

WHAT WAS EATING MICHELE, NICK WONDERED.

Not that the woman ever had what one would term a "sunny disposition." Like himself, she was too single-minded for that. But this morning she seemed particularly cranky. Had he inadvertently done something to set her off? It was quite clear she'd been itching for a fight back in the cottage.

Why?

Frustrated, Nick guided the pickup to a stop safely outside the stables and cast a glance her way. She sat staring out the passenger window, her arms folded across her chest, her stubborn chin jutting forward, for all practical purposes, closing him out.

Just when their relationship had been making some head-way, she'd decided to fall back on her hardline defenses. Typical cop.

He recalled the night before with a half-smile. They'd made a pretty darn good team, breaking into the vet's office, defeating the watchdog, obtaining Whirlwind's blood sample.

The intensity of the experience had produced some extremely sexual thoughts in him. And those provocative few minutes in the bathroom when she'd tenderly ministered his wounds, well, whew! No matter how much Michele Mallory might want to deny it, she was as hot for him as he was for her. Even now, simply thinking about her passion caused a heated rush to flood his body.

Nick knew that if he ever coaxed her to bed, the chemistry between them would be sheer dynamite. He had no doubt she'd be his kind of lover—lusty and robust. Her kisses told him that Michele would go at sex the same way she tackled life, no holds barred, danger be damned.

A violent shiver ran through him at the idea.

Knock it off, Nickerson. It was hard enough holding back his sexual urges for the sake of the investigation, the last thing he needed was to dwell on the subject.

Without a word, Nick opened the door and got out of the truck. The paddocks were abuzz with activity even though the sun hadn't broken the horizon. The air smelled fresh, clean, cheerful.

Elvira breezed a Thoroughbred on the track. Steve Bradshaw harnessed a quarter horse to the walker. A stable hand hosed off an Arabian mare who had apparently just completed a run. Inside the barn, several horses were chomping at a breakfast of high protein rolled oats and multivitamins.

In a matter of minutes, Nick found himself caught up in the daily chores of caring for temperamental racehorses. He threw himself into the work, grateful for any distraction. He had to keep his mind on his job and off Michele Mallory.

At nine-thirty, once most of the horses had been fed, watered, exercised, and doctored, Nick and the rest of the hands took a break. He'd lost track of Michele early on and couldn't stop himself from scanning the ranch in search of her.

Spotting Steve Bradshaw standing near Whirlwind's stall, Nick sauntered over.

"Hey," he greeted the other man. "How's the gelding this morning?"

"Groggy." Steve narrowed his eyes. "Can't figure out what happened last night."

"Pretty wild," Nick concurred. "It was as if Whirlwind was high on amphetamines."

"Yeah." Bradshaw turned his face away, concentrating on rubbing down the sluggish iron-gray.

Nick studied the lanky stable hand, trying hard to decipher his role in the incident. Did Bradshaw know something? Had he doped Whirlwind? For what reason?

"Have you seen my wife?" Nick asked.

The word "wife" came so easily, it startled him. To his dismay, he found the idea of being married to Michele not the least bit unpleasant. He twisted the plain, gold wedding band on his ring finger. What was happening to him? He was not the marrying kind. His ex-wife could testify to that. Work would always come first in his life, even with someone as exciting as Michele Mallory.

"She said somethin' about trying to ride Jet."

"The stallion?" The mere idea of Michele mounting that powerful beast had the hairs on his arms standing at attention and goosebumps blanketing his skin.

"Yep. Jim told her she's crazy, but your wife has got a stubborn streak a mile wide."

"Tell me about it," Nick muttered.

"Bet she's quite a handful," Steve smirked.

"Where's the stallion?" Nick asked, ignoring the weasel-faced man's innuendo.

"North paddock."

Nick took off, his heart thumping. How could Michele do something so foolish as riding an untamed stallion? What if she got hurt? Where would that leave the investigation?

He had a fleeting urge to take her over his knee and paddle her fanny. That image only served to fuel his hunger for her. He'd give a month's wages to feel her firm, high breasts pressed against his thighs, her delectable bottom cupped in his hands.

"Dammit, Nick, you've gotta stop thinking like this," he chided himself as he stalked across the field. He reached a gate and climbed over.

Finding her was no problem. A crowd of stable hands lined the wooden paddock fence, respectfully silent, all eyes trained on his "wife." Nick inched closer until he stood next to Elvira.

Michele had backed the stallion into a corner. The high-strung creature stood very still, his ears pricked at attention.

Moving painstakingly slow, Michele approached from the side, cooing soft, low words of comfort. What would it take, Nick wondered, to have her speak to him in such tender tones.

She extended her left arm, an apple as a peace offering resting on her open palm. In her right hand, she clutched a bridle behind her back, hiding it from Jet.

"There now, that's a good boy." She crept closer, the nervous stallion watching her every move. Bravely, she met the horse's gaze and kept advancing.

The stallion tossed his head and made a move to turn, but Michele countered with her own body language, reassuring the steed.

"Hey, now, don't be afraid," she murmured.

"Michele's good," Elvira whispered to Nick, standing on her tiptoes to see better. "I've never even tried to ride Jet."

At last, Michele drew near enough so that the stallion lightly nipped the apple from her palm. She waited while he chewed, snorted, and then sniffed her hand.

If she ever treated him with such patient understanding, Nick would willingly eat from her hand as well. Michele Mallory might be a whiz with horses, but when it came to people, her skills left a lot to be desired.

He watched as she ran a hand along Jet's back, the bridle still hidden behind her. She wrapped an arm around Jet's withers and leaned her weight against him.

A collective sigh went up from the stable hands.

Jim Hollis came up behind Nick. Turning, Nick nodded to the older man.

"Your wife is a hell of a woman," the trainer observed.

"Yeah," Nick replied gruffly. "She is."

They made a great team, the two of them. Was it possible that they might have a future together once this investigation was complete?

"You're a lucky man, Nick," Hollis said, a wistful note creeping into his voice. "You treasure that girl, you hear? I was too busy with horses to pay any attention to my wife. Sure was a shock when she took Jenna and left me. Don't let that happen to you."

Nick nodded, not knowing what else to say. If Michele were his, he'd do his level best to hang on to her.

"If little Katie hadn't gotten sick, I don't know if I would ever have mended fences with Jenna and my ex-wife," Jim continued, a pensive, faraway look on his face. "I used to think horses were all that mattered. Now, with Katie needing a liver transplant, I've finally realized how selfish I've been, putting animals ahead of my loved ones."

"Look." Elvira excitedly tugged Nick's sleeve. "Michele's got the bit in Jet's mouth."

Nick looked up. Sure enough, while Hollis had been talking, Michele had not only managed to get the bridle on Jet, but she was waving at a cowboy to hand her the saddle.

In a matter of minutes, Michele had saddled the horse and climbed astride the massive creature. Like a fairy-tale princess, she paraded around the paddock, the reins held tightly in her hands as she skillfully controlled the stallion. Her blond ponytail bounced behind her like a jaunty flag, her cheeks flushed rosy with excitement. Admiration for her swelled Nick's chest. Heaven help him, he was a goner.

Overwhelmed by his emotions, Nick turned away. "I better go start lunch," he muttered to Elvira.

"I'll help you," the cheerful jockey offered, doffing her helmet and running a hand through her short, red curls.

"Great," Nick said, distracted. His brain was whirling with visions of Michele. What was it about Mallory that had so effectively captured his attention? Could he possibly be falling in love?

Pushing the unsettling thought to the back of his mind, Nick started across the pasture, Elvira trotting beside him like an enthusiastic pup.

MICHELE SMILED TRIUMPHANTLY. HER GAZE SCANNED THE gathered stable hands. Her eyes landed on Nick's retreating figure. Had he been here all along? Had he seen her conquer the infamous stallion? She realized with a jolt exactly how much she wanted his approval. When had Nickerson's opinion begun to matter so much?

She watched Nick walk away, Elvira skipping along beside him. He placed a hand on the little jockey's shoulder, and Michele gritted her teeth. Could Nick be interested in the woman? She knew Elvira was fascinated by him. Her stomach roiled at the notion, and Michele feared she might be sick.

Angered by irrational jealousy, Michele threw caution to the wind and gave Jet more rein. Gleefully, the stallion tossed his head.

"Open the paddock gate," she snapped at Jim Hollis.

"I don't think that's such a good idea, Michele," the trainer said.

"I know what I'm doing," she insisted. "Open the gate."

"Suit yourself, but don't say I didn't warn you." Hollis swung open the gate and stood to one side.

Michele kneed the stallion. With a spirited toss of his head, Jet took off across the field, galloping straight for Nick and Elvira.

How dare Nickerson put his arm on the jockey's shoulder in public, Michele fumed. Even if he was a typical Neanderthal male, as a law enforcement officer, the man should have more respect for their undercover assignment. They were supposed to be newlyweds, for crying out loud.

She flew past Nick and Elvira without looking back, the hole in her heart growing larger with each thundering step Jet took.

What did it matter? After the assignment was over, she'd never see Nickerson again. Good riddance. The man was nothing but a royal pain in the butt.

So why did her chest feel tighter than a rubber band pulled to the breaking point? Why couldn't she stop thinking about the way he smelled, the rich sound of his voice, the spectacular taste of his full lips?

Get a grip, Mallory. He's just a guy. But no matter how much her rational mind might wish to deny her attraction to him, her body had other plans.

Every time she closed her eyes, she saw that smooth expanse of tanned, muscular chest, that narrow waist, those brawny legs. She ached for his kisses, pined for his touch, grieved to hear him call her "babe."

But most of all, she thirsted for the passionate nature that was exclusively Nick Nickerson.

Michele groaned. Somewhere along the way, she'd come to care too deeply for this man who commanded everyone's attention when he waltzed into a room. She was attracted to his power, his courage, his joie de vivre. Last night, he'd fought a vicious dog for her. Today, she feared she might be falling for precisely the same sort of guy she'd struggled her whole life to avoid. A man just like her authoritative, controlling father.

And she was a woman far too much like her stubborn, autocratic mother. Look what had happened to her parents' disastrous union. While she had been caught in the middle. A pawn in her parents' ugly game of "Who's got the upper hand?"

Michele had sworn if she ever married, she'd fall in love with a kind, gentle, mild-mannered fellow, not a rebellious, domineering, aggressive he-man. A relationship with Nickerson would be like lighting a match near an incendiary device. Dangerous and stupid.

By the time her anger and dismay had dwindled to embers, Michele wheeled Jet around and trotted him back to the stables. The stallion had been a prince, challenging yet agreeable. Too bad Nickerson wasn't as easily tamed.

❦ 13 ❦

Michele unsaddled Jet and handed him over to a groom to be cooled down. Then, making sure she was unobserved, crossed the exercise yard and slipped into the building that headquartered the Triple Fork's offices.

Jim Hollis's door was unlocked. Michele pushed it open and trod inside, her boots echoing against the plywood flooring. A ceiling fan whirled overhead. Cigarette butts lay curled in an ashtray on the scarred desk. Metal file cabinets lined one wall.

Unsure exactly what she was looking for, Michele quickly perused the file labels. Racing schedules, jockey engagements, medical regimes.

This could take forever.

She plunked down in the swivel chair parked in front of the desk. It creaked in protest. Pictures of Hollis's granddaughter, Katie, were prominently displayed in decorative frames. Surely, Jim had nothing to do with drugging horses. He loved animals far too much to jeopardize them or his career.

Feeling like a treacherous snake, she pulled open a drawer and peered inside. Pencils, a stapler, half a pack of spearmint chewing gum. The next drawer yielded little more—a condition book, two horse magazines, and a rusty horseshoe.

In the last drawer, she found the Triple Fork's training log. Leafing through the register, she scanned for the names of horses who had been underdogs in their respective races but had pulled from behind to win.

She leaned back in the chair. The toe of her boot came in contact with something under the table. Lowering her head, she peered at a cardboard packet taped to the bottom of the desk.

Her pulse accelerated. Nervously, she removed the package and stared down at the innocuous envelope as if it were a loaded gun.

Dare she open it?

Michele cleared her throat. What choice did she have? She had to find out. What could be inside?

Carefully, she peeled back the tape and dumped the contents on the desk.

Canceled checks flitted out, dozens of them. Drawn on a Swiss bank account and made out to Jim Hollis.

Her breath caught in her lungs. With a cry of dismay, she dropped the packet.

The checks had been signed by Mario Martuchi, the renowned mafia henchman. The first one in the stack was made out for fifteen thousand dollars and dated three months earlier.

Michele brought a hand to her mouth. Jim Hollis was involved!

Unable to believe the evidence staring her in the face, she gulped. Nick had to be told right away.

With fumbling fingers, she stuffed the checks back into the envelope. A few wafted away from her, caught in the updraft from the ceiling fan. Michele scurried around the office retrieving them.

Once she had all the checks back in the envelope, she got on her knees to tape the packet back to the desk.

Her heart pounded; her mouth went dry. She felt light-headed, still unable to believe Jim Hollis was involved.

She'd been so sure it was Steve Bradshaw or Dr. Felix or even Elvira.

Just as she got the packet securely fixed to the bottom of the desk drawer, the office door creaked open.

She popped up like a guilty jack-in-the-box and found herself staring face-to-face with Jim's granddaughter, Katie.

"Hi," the little girl greeted Michele, her blue eyes wide and sad despite the smile on her face. She clutched a rag doll in one hand.

"Uh... hi."

"Whatcha doing under Pappaw's desk?"

Michele scrambled to her feet and snatched a pencil off the trainer's desk. "Dropped my pencil," she explained, chagrined at having been busted by a four-year-old, but relieved it wasn't Jim Hollis standing in the doorway.

"Katie," a voice called from outside. "Where are you?"

Michele edged away from the desk, still smiling when Jenna appeared.

"There you are." Jenna took Katie's arm and returned Michele's smile. "How are you, Mrs. Prescott?"

For a moment Michele forgot that she was Mrs. Prescott. "Fine," she said. "And please, call me Michele."

"Come on, Katie, let's go eat hot dogs with Pappaw." Jenna guided Katie out the door. "Are you going to join us?" The other woman eyed her curiously.

Michele knew she was wondering the same thing her young daughter had been bold enough to ask. What was she doing in Jim's office?

"Sure."

Not knowing what else to do, Michele followed Katie and Jenna out the door and across the exercise yard. Somehow, she had to get Nick alone and bring him back here to show him what she'd found. The implication weighed heavily on her heart. She did not want Jim Hollis to be the culprit. He was a nice man with a very sick little granddaughter.

Not too nice, a voice in the back of her head insisted, *he's been illegally doping horses for big bucks.*

The three of them tromped into the house, Katie chattering to her mother about her pony.

The kitchen buzzed with activity. Cowboys moved card tables out the back door. Elvira arranged condiments on a serving tray. Jim Hollis hefted a cooler of cold drinks. Steve Bradshaw carried a bag of corn chips under one arm, potato chips under the other. A large watermelon rested on the counter.

Amazing, Michele marveled. Nick had conned the whole ranch into helping him prepare lunch.

Nick stood at the stove, dishing up grilled frankfurters on a platter, an apron proclaiming Cowboys Do it with Their Boots On tied around his waist.

Nick.

Michele's heart catapulted into her throat at the sight of her undercover husband. Staring at him, she forgot about Jim Hollis, canceled checks, racehorse doping, everything. For that brief moment, Nick completely dominated her thoughts.

He turned to see her. A smile lit his face, so sincere it warmed her like summer sunshine. Heavens, he was handsome with that scruffy, black hair tangling down his neck and those dark eyes glimmering impudently.

"What's going on?" Michele asked, walking over to the stove. She frowned, wrinkling her nose against the heat emanating from the grill.

Nick brazened a wink. "Since the north wind kicked up nice and breezy, we decided to eat outside."

"A picnic, a picnic," Katie exclaimed, clapping her hands and twirling around the room on her heels.

Michele took a step back, suddenly embarrassed with the realization that everyone was watching them.

Nick slid an arm around her shoulders and leaned into the curve of her body, effectively preventing her escape. She sucked in a gasp. His body generated enough electricity to illuminate Austin for a year.

"Did you enjoy riding Jet?" he asked, low and throaty.

"Uh-huh," Michele answered, her brain jumbled by his propinquity.

"You looked pretty awesome out there," he whispered. "Like a rodeo queen on parade."

His words flattered. Michele didn't want to admit it, but she lapped up his praise like a puppy at a water bowl.

Don't read anything into this, Mallory, she warned herself. Nickerson was just playing a role. True, he wanted her body, but that didn't make him husband material, not by a long shot. Besides, she was not looking for a husband, anyway.

His grip tightened. He smelled delicious, like onions and mustard and sweet pickle relish. Common sense told her to run. Her instincts told her to pick a fight. She did neither. Instead, Michele simply enjoyed the pleasant feelings surging through her.

Too quickly, her mind conjured an intimate scene in the future where they might be standing in their own kitchen, without an audience. Nick would nuzzle her neck and unbutton her blouse. She would turn into his kiss, arching her back, urging him to suckle her breasts.

Images of heated oil and melted candle wax oozed through her brain. Gulping, she licked her lips.

What was happening to her?

This has to stop, Michele. Her father's voice, stern and accusing, rumbled through her mind.

Why? She mentally argued with the logical, authoritative side of her brain—the side that parroted her father's strict standards. Why couldn't she allow herself to fantasize about Nickerson? Where was the harm?

The harm lay in making a fool of herself over a man who was only attracted to her on a physical level. Nick's playboy nature was renowned throughout the department. He'd told her himself he wasn't marriage material, and she refused to become just another passing conquest.

"Mind taking these out to the picnic table?" Nick asked, removing his arm from around her shoulders and handing her three packages of hot dog buns.

"Pretty sneaky, Nick, getting the ranch hands to help you make lunch."

"No one can resist my charms," he said, too low for anyone else to hear.

"Except me."

"Even you, Mish. Like it or not, one of these days I'm going to get to you."

"Better not hold your breath; a blue face could greatly reduce your sex appeal."

"That's what I like about you, Mish. Feisty as hell." With that, he picked up the platter of frankfurters and strutted out the door.

Grumbling under her breath about his cocky arrogance, Michele joined everyone at the picnic tables. She made a conscious effort to sit as far from Nick as possible, positioning herself at the end of the table between Elvira and Jenna.

"Boy," Elvira exclaimed, squirting mustard on her hot dog. "Eating outside was a great idea, Nick."

"Thanks." Nick grinned, his eyes catching Michele's.

Quickly, she looked away.

"How long have you and Nick been married?" Jenna asked once Michele had settled in with her plate.

"Um..." Michele hesitated, trying to remember their cover story. "Three months."

"Ah, you guys are still honeymooning," Jenna said.

"Three months of pure heaven," Nick piped up from where he was sitting next to Jim Hollis, little Katie wedged between them.

Did he have to lay it on so thick? Michele scowled and concentrated on her lunch.

The conversation drifted to talk about the upcoming races and Whirlwind's condition. Michele sneaked a glance at Jim Hollis, but his face was unreadable. She needed to tell Nick about the envelope she'd found under Hollis's desk, but she hadn't had the opportunity. After lunch, she would offer to help him clean up, and they could talk then.

"Who's ready for watermelon?" Nick asked when most everyone had finished their hot dogs.

"Me, me, me," Katie trilled.

"You want to help me bring it outside?" Nick asked, taking the little girl by the hand.

"Yes."

They returned a few minutes later, Nick carrying the watermelon and a knife, Katie clutching paper plates.

The group ate watermelon, the crisp, clean aroma scenting the air. A wistful sweetness lingered on Michele's tongue.

Nick nudged Katie with his elbow. "I challenge you to a watermelon seed spitting contest."

Katie giggled. "Okay."

"Nick!" Michele chided, appalled. "Don't be encouraging her to spit!"

"It's okay," Jenna said, laying a hand on Michele's arm and

speaking low. "I suppose I should be stricter with her, but somehow I can't bring myself to discipline her. Who knows how much longer she might be with us."

What a sobering thought. Michele's heart somersaulted at the idea of poor little Katie's illness. How dreadful it must be for Jenna.

"How is your husband dealing with Katie's illness?" Michele asked.

Jenna shook her head. "Katie's dad took off at the first sign of trouble."

Michele narrowed her eyes. How could any man leave his family in their time of need? How would Nickerson react in a similar situation? Would he, too, turn tail and run?

No, Michele thought as she watched him with the child. Nick was too much of a protector to abandon those depending on him.

Nick spit a seed onto the grass.

"I can do better than that!" Katie crowed.

"Oh, yeah?" He lightly tickled the girl under her arms.

Katie's childish laughter filled the air, tugging unexpectedly at some longing deep within Michele. She'd told herself she didn't need a husband or children to feel complete, that police work was enough for her. But was that true? Suddenly an empty chasm yawned inside her chest.

"Your husband is great with her," Jenna said, sipping a glass of ginger ale. "Are you two planning on starting a family soon?"

Michele pondered the question. Children with Nick? In her mind's eye, she could see a little girl with Nick's dark curls or an impish boy with his teasing smile.

"We're going to see what happens," she replied to Jenna, disconcerted by the wall of tears building behind her eyes. Now, why on earth was she feeling teary?

"You two will make gorgeous babies." Jenna grinned.

"Thanks," Michele said, unnerved by the thought of having a child with Nick.

Nick and Katie had given up watermelon seed spitting to play Ring Around the Rosy in the Saint Augustine grass. He danced the child around in a circle, and they landed on the ground with a soft plop. One of Katie's pigtails popped free from her red hair ribbon.

"Come here, honey, I'll redo your hair," Jenna called out.

Katie shook her head, looked up at Nick, and extended her ribbon toward him. "You do it," she insisted.

"I'm not very good at fixing little girls' pigtails," Nick said.

"You'll do fine." Katie nodded, sounding extremely grown-up.

A tenderness unlike anything Michele had ever felt stole over her as she watched Nick awkwardly retie Katie's hair. Of course, the pigtails didn't match once he had finished. One lay neatly pinned while the other stuck out from her head at an odd angle—but he and Katie both beamed widely at his handiwork.

One day, Nick would make a wonderful father for some lucky woman's child.

Why can't I be that woman? Determinedly, Michele pushed the thought from her mind. How many times did she have to remind herself that she and Nickerson were just too much alike to ever make a go of a relationship? They'd be at each other's throats before the preacher could say, "You may kiss the bride."

"I'll take her off your hands," Jenna said to Nick, pushing back from the table and retrieving Katie. "Thanks for entertaining her."

"My pleasure." Nick smiled.

"Come on, honey." Jenna took her daughter by the hand. "Let's go look at the horses."

"I'll help you clean up," Michele said to Nick, as everyone finished their meal and scattered back to work.

"You're offering to help me? To what do I owe this unexpected pleasure?"

Michele glanced over her shoulder to where Jim Hollis and Jenna had taken Katie over to the paddock. "I found something in Hollis's office," she whispered.

"What?" Immediately, Nick was at attention, the teasing light vanishing from his eyes. "Why didn't you tell me?"

"How could I? You've been surrounded by people."

"In the house," Nick said, scooping up the empty platter and empty cola cans. "Now."

His commanding tone grated on her, but she followed him inside, the screen door creaking shut behind them.

"Spill it, Wife." He slid the platter across the counter and placed his hands on his hips.

"I found an envelope of canceled checks hidden under the bottom of Jim's desk."

"And?"

"They were made out to him from Mario Martuchi."

"The mafia lowlife who's been indicted on charges of race-horse tampering in Louisiana."

"You got it."

Disappointment settled over Nick's face. "I didn't want it to be Jim," he said softly.

"Me either, but the evidence is pretty self-explanatory."

"Show me," Nick said, untying the cowboy apron and tossing it on the kitchen cabinet. "Let's get this case solved. I'm ready to go home."

Home.

Michele should be relieved to have the case come to an end. Instead, she felt a strange hollowness deep within her at the notion of her empty apartment.

🦋 14 🦋

Nick and Michele went back outside. Jim Hollis, his daughter, and granddaughter were still in the paddock.

They dodged around the back of the stables, darting furtive glances as they went. "I feel like a spy," she said.

"You are. Come on." Nick stalked to the building and turned the doorknob.

They entered Jim's office. The air was dead, motionless, the ceiling fan silent.

"Keep watch," Nick said, striding across the room to the desk while Michele hovered near the door.

He disappeared behind the desk.

"Hurry," Michele urged.

"Where is it?" Nick's head popped up.

"Taped to the underside of the top drawer."

"I don't see it," Nick groused. "Are you sure?"

"Oh, here." Michele heaved an exasperated sigh and marched over beside Nick. She ran a hand along the desk's underbelly but encountered no resistance. She'd taped the envelope to the spot where she'd found it, hadn't she? Dropping to her hands and knees, her shoulder banged into Nick's.

Trying hard to resist the ripple of desire racing through her, Michele tilted her head and looked at the bottom of the desk.

Nothing.

She rocked back on her heels and met Nick's hard-edged gaze.

"It's gone," she said.

⚜

"THE BLOOD SAMPLE TESTED NEGATIVE," LIEUTENANT Charboneau said between bites of a double meat cheeseburger. It was Wednesday, and they were sitting in a booth at the Dairy Diner in Marfa, thirty miles from Rascal.

"Whirlwind was doped," Michele insisted. "You should have seen how he acted."

"Michele's right." Nickerson nodded. "The horse was wild, crazy, unmanageable."

"So." Charboneau dabbed his chin with a paper napkin. "You think the trainer is the culprit?"

"Does Doris know you indulge in those?" Michele asked, referring to Charboneau's wife. She wrinkled her nose and waved a hand at his plate.

"What she doesn't know won't hurt her," her boss replied. "And don't try to change the subject. Explain to me again, Mallory, how you neglected to confiscate such crucial evidence when it presented itself to you."

She couldn't tell Charboneau how her mindless attraction to Nick had derailed her. She was ashamed for not commandeering at least one check from the envelope of canceled checks when she'd had the chance. "I made a mistake, Lieutenant."

"I'm disappointed in you, Mallory." Charboneau polished off his cheeseburger and wadded up his napkin. "I've come to expect such thorough work from you."

"It wasn't Michele's fault," Nick said, rising to her defense. "She was interrupted. Besides, the canceled checks don't really prove anything, and even if Hollis is accepting money from the mob, that doesn't necessarily mean he's doping horses."

"Thanks, Nick," Michele said softly. "But the lieutenant is right. I should have told you about the envelope right away, instead of giving someone the opportunity to get rid of the evidence."

Charboneau looked from Nick to Michele and back again. "Maybe it was a bad idea, sending you two on assignment together."

Michele looked down at her hands. Nick's plain, gold wedding band encircled her finger. Except it wasn't really Nick's ring, and they weren't genuinely married.

Charboneau would never know the impact this investigation was having on her. The last few days spent posing as Nick's wife raised all sorts of sticky issues. Issues she'd put on the back burner to deal with sometime in the distant future, issues like marriage and love and children.

"Okay. Enough recrimination. What's done is done." Charboneau steepled his fingers. "Let's review what we know so far and make further plans."

"Whirlwind was most likely doped with untraceable amphetamines. What we don't know is why," Nick said.

"Maybe they were testing it out?" Michele arched an eyebrow. "Giving the drug a trial run before the races this weekend."

Charboneau nodded. "Maybe."

"The head groom, Steve Bradshaw, was involved in shady dealings with the Triple Fork's previous ranch manager, Lance

Kane," Michele added. "But that's strictly hearsay from Elvira Montrose."

"And Michele found the envelope of canceled checks under Hollis's desk," Nick said. "That's all we've got to go on."

"Maybe those checks were completely legitimate," Michele mused, hating the idea that Jim Hollis was responsible for the dopings.

"Then why were they taped to the bottom of the desk drawer?" Charboneau asked. "Sounds to me like Mr. Hollis is trying to hide something."

Nick shook his head. "It's hard to believe Hollis would jeopardize his livelihood."

"Money"—Charboneau rubbed his thumb and forefingers together—"can be a powerful motivator. Without the canceled checks, we have no evidence, so I suggest you two get back to the ranch and bring me cold, hard proof."

"Yes, sir," Michele mumbled, feeling foolish for having neglected her duties.

Spirits dragging, she followed Nick out to the truck, leaving the lieutenant happily licking a soft-serve ice-cream cone.

"Chin up," Nick said, chucking a fist lightly under her chin before climbing into the pickup.

"I blew it." Michele shook her head. "Like a rookie trooper."

"You're very hard on yourself," he commented, snapping his seat belt into place.

"Yeah, well, I was taught by the best. I never could live up to my father's high standards."

"Want to talk about it?"

Michele slid Nick a sideways glance. Did she really want to open up to him? Telling secrets would deepen the bond between them. She'd already let her guard down way too low.

Was she ready for the next logical progression in their relationship?

"No."

"All right." He didn't say another word, just turned on the headlights and drove out of the parking lot.

Michele settled back in her seat and listened to the prolonged silence. She hitched in a breath, hoping to corral her mind. But to her dismay, her emotions broke forth and came gushing out in an unstoppable flow of words.

"I was never good enough," she whispered. "Not for my mother and most certainly not for my father. I should have been smarter, prettier, braver, stronger. No matter what I did, it wasn't enough. If I made A's, my father wanted to know why I hadn't made A-pluses. If I placed second in a riding competition, my mother demanded to know why I wasn't first."

Nick reached out a hand and laid it on her knee. He said nothing, just waited for her to continue, the warm pressure of his hand fortifying her.

"As I tried to please first one parent, then the other, they'd fight over me. My father pulling me in one direction, my mother dragging me in the opposite."

"Sounds rough."

"Believe me, having two headstrong parents makes for a chaotic family life. And after the divorce, things got even worse. Finally, I couldn't take it anymore and rebelled against both of them. When I entered the police academy, they both went ballistic. It was the first time I ever felt truly in control of my life, and I loved the feeling of freedom."

Nick squeezed her knee, comforting her.

"Back there with Charboneau, I felt like I was a little girl again, displeasing my father." Michele's voice cracked, and she had to stop talking to swallow back the tears threatening to roll down her cheeks. All those years of fighting for her own identity and she could still be quelled by her father's disapproval. "A psychiatrist would probably say that's why I'm such a stickler for rules. Sometimes I wish I could simply let go and enjoy the moment. Like you do."

She studied Nick's face. He appeared relaxed, one hand draped over the steering wheel, his posture casual. But his eyes were bright and sharp.

"It's a role I've perfected," Nick said. "It's why I'm so good at undercover assignments. I learned a long time ago to adapt to the environment. That's how I control my world. Pretend you belong. Act as if you're the top dog, and most of the time people let you lead."

"Ah, come on. You're so self-assured."

"So are you, Michele. To the outside observer. That's what counts, the public image."

"What about the private Nick?" she asked, immensely intrigued and more than a little aroused by the sweet kneading motion he was applying to her knee.

"He's a hard guy to get to know."

"No kidding. We were on assignment for three weeks together, and you never said a word about your personal life."

"Neither did you."

"I didn't think it was professional."

"And I didn't want to get involved."

"Guess we're two of a kind, huh?"

"Looks like it."

What would she find if she took the time to delve head-long into the man that was Nick Nickerson? He was coura-geous, she already knew that. And strong-willed. But what was he like in an intimate relationship? Would he be a compassionate lover, tender and understanding? Or would he be bold and forceful, taking his passion the way he tackled life, committed, commanding, audacious?

Michele quivered.

His kisses told her probably the latter, and that frightened her more than she cared to admit. His blazing inner fire stirred something monumental inside her. No matter how she might wish to deny it, she was falling in love with Nick. And a match of two such ardent personalities could only end in disaster. Her parents' relationship was a prime example.

Despite the frantic urging of her baser instincts, she could not allow her physical desires free rein with this man. She had to find a way to kill her growing attraction or face the ultimate broken heart.

⚜

THAT NIGHT, MICHELE PULLED A KNEE-LENGTH SLEEP SHIRT over her head and stared at herself in the bathroom mirror. Her hair was disheveled, her cheeks flushed hot, her lips full and hungry. She wanted Nick's kisses. Now. Sharp, fiery, delicious.

Gritting her teeth, she glared at her reflection. Somehow, she had to fight these yearnings. She could not afford the luxury of any more slipups. Her career hinged on her ability to control her emotions.

But how did you stop yourself from falling in love?

She heard Nick bumping around in the other room and wondered what he was doing. Everything about him aroused her curiosity. From his insouciant countenance to his steely composure under pressure, she could not seem to channel her attention to more appropriate subjects. Nick Nickerson dominated her brain like gambling dominated horseracing.

He was an addiction. A drug. A habit so attractive, she couldn't refuse. But resist she must. Her fascination with him was as destructive as any other compulsion.

"Just stop it, Michele," she growled at her image in the small mirror. "Remember self-control."

She washed her face and brushed her teeth, dragging out the bedtime ritual in hopes Nick would be sound asleep by the time she finished.

Finally, when she could postpone the inevitable no longer, she stepped out into the hallway and switched off the bathroom light behind her.

"Michele."

His voice called to her from the shadows—deep, throaty, and oh so masculine. She imagined him sprawled out on the queen-size bed, waiting for her. She shivered.

"Yes?"

"Come here."

Don't go, don't go, don't go, her mind screamed. But her body had other plans.

"Mish." Nick's voice drew her like a sacrificial virgin to Dracula's lair.

She tiptoed into the bedroom and paused in the doorway, her heart thundering, helpless to turn away.

He lay stretched out like a predatory cat, propped up on one elbow, his face hidden by shadows. His naked chest rose and fell in a steady, controlled rhythm as if he were completely relaxed. Yet she sensed he was on full alert, ready to pounce at a moment's notice.

"Y-y-yes," she stammered, awash in a sudden heat. Perspiration dotted her upper lip, and the nightshirt clung to her bare breasts.

Holy smokes, she was in trouble.

෧෴ඁ

NICK STARED AT MICHELE, ARRESTED BY HER BEAUTY. Moonglow spilling in from the curtainless window silhouetted her in a pale, glimmering light. She was breathtaking, her womanly curves outlined against the thin cotton material of her sleep shirt. His body responded instantly to the visual stimulation.

"You can't sleep on the couch," he said, struggling to keep his voice on an even keel. If he was going to convince her to spend the night in the bed, she could not guess at the intensity of his arousal.

"Of course I can," she retorted, flipping a lock of that glorious red-gold hair over her slender shoulder.

"No," he insisted. "It's much too uncomfortable. Last night, a spring kept poking me in the back, and I ended up sleeping on the floor."

"It's not that bad." She shrugged.

"There's no reason we can't share this bed." He patted the mattress.

Who was he kidding? There were a million reasons why they shouldn't share the same bed. The number one reason being he doubted he could keep his hands off her.

Nick swallowed. He prided himself on his sense of control. He was disciplined. Hadn't his stint in the Marine Corps proven that? And intrepid—he'd thrown his old man out of the house at age fifteen. Surely, he could spend the night next to a gorgeous woman without groping her like a randy teenager.

Except Michele Mallory wasn't just any woman. And the way she made him feel defied rational thought.

"I don't think that's such a good idea," she said.

He rolled onto his stomach to camouflage his desire. "I promise, this is only for comfort's sake. I won't touch you." *Unless you want me to.*

No, no, no. They had an investigation to conclude. He couldn't even dream of seducing Michele until they were no longer partners. Especially after they'd fumbled the ball over Hollis. And they'd both been at fault on that deal. If he hadn't been so intent on showing her up by throwing a picnic for the ranch hands, Michele wouldn't have had to wait so long to tell him about the checks.

"I'm going to sleep on the couch," she said, taking a step backward.

"Wait." Damn, why did his word come out so eager? "Then you take the bed, and I'll sleep on the couch."

"Oh, no." She shook her head.

"But I insist." Nick felt like a dummy arguing with her while lying on his stomach. Quickly, he flipped over and sat up, making sure to keep the sheet bunched loosely about his waist.

"Please. No."

She sounded almost desperate. He expected her to read him the riot act, and instead she was pleading with him. Where was the tough-as-nails Michele he'd come to know and love?

Love?

Glory. What was he thinking? He couldn't be in love with her, could he? If the rapid acceleration of his pulse were any indication, yes, he could.

Whoa. Wait a minute. Slow down. He wasn't cut out for love and marriage. He'd tried it once, and he'd been a miserable failure as a husband.

But that was with your ex, not Michele, an obnoxious voice in the back of his mind argued. He and his ex-wife had nothing in common whereas he and Michele were both dedicated law enforcement officers. Things could be different.

But he was happy as a single, carefree bachelor. He didn't want to relinquish control of his life and climb on that wild roller coaster ride of love. Uh-uh. No way. No how. Forget it.

Nickerson, you 're in deep horse manure.

"I'm sleeping on the couch," Michele said firmly.

"Come on," he coaxed. "What's the big deal? You sleep on

the right side of the bed; I sleep on the left. Never the twain shall meet, and we'll both get a good night's sleep."

He waited for her heated retort, but none came. Raising a hand to his forehead, Nick realized he was sweating. Michele was right. It would be incredibly stupid to share the same bed. If the way he was feeling right now was any indication, somebody was going to get hurt, and that somebody was most likely him.

"All right," she acquiesced at last, leaving Nick stunned. He'd never expected her to concede.

Three days ago, he would have been able to pinpoint her every response, knew exactly how she might handle a given situation. But now? He hadn't a clue.

Lacing his palms together behind his head, he lay back down and stared at the ceiling. Could she hear the crazy rumbling of his heart?

❧ 15 ❧

Michele crept closer.

Nick closed his eyes and swallowed past the mountain in his throat. How long had it been since a woman had roused him to these heights? Ever? Never?

Stiffly, she eased down on the edge of the mattress. "Do you promise not to touch me?" she whispered into the darkness.

"Promise."

A heavenly cloud of cinnamon enveloped as she climbed between the covers. Oh, Lord, this was a bad, bad idea. Nick turned on his side, away from her, his face to the wall. How could he sleep with a goddess curled up in bed next to him?

He heard her ragged intake of breath and realized she was as nervous as he. Newlyweds on their wedding night could not have been as jittery.

"Nick," she whispered, as soft and enticing as a fresh sea breeze.

"Uh-huh?"

"There's something I've always wanted to ask you, and since we're sharing a bed, I thought this might be the time."

Her question piqued his curiosity. Was she wondering if he were disease free? If he used protection? His pulse quickened at the notion. Could she be thinking about...nah...no way. "You can ask me anything."

"How did you get that scar?"

He rubbed his jaw. He supposed he could lie and tell her some dramatic story about how he got hurt on the job, but this was Michele and she was asking with sincerity.

"My brothers and I were playing The Three Musketeers and things got out of hand."

"How old were you?"

"Eleven." He rubbed his jaw again, remembering all that blood spewing about the living room of the trailer house where they lived.

His old man had been furious and whipped them all for horsing around. He refused to spend money on a hospital visit and had taped up Nick's wound with butterfly strips, but Nick decided to leave out that part.

"May I ask you something else?"

"Fire away."

"What's your real name?"

"Huh?" That caught him off guard.

"Everybody calls you 'Nick' but that's just short for Nickerson, isn't it?"

"Yeah."

"So what's your real name?"

"Promise not to laugh?"

"Is it that bad?" She giggled.

"Hey, you're laughing already."

How great it felt to lie here beside her, gently joking. As if they were a long-married couple sharing the events of their day.

What he wouldn't give to scoop her into his arms and drive her crazy with foreplay. He wanted to kiss her eyes, her nose, her throat. He'd like to trail his tongue down her satiny skin until he reached those full, perky breasts. He longed to massage her back, knead her into a pliant puddle of heated putty.

"I won't laugh," she said, and he could tell she was forcing her lips together to keep from chortling out loud.

The fact that he made her laugh warmed Nick clean to the bone. Usually, Michele was far too serious. He'd never guessed at this playful dimension to her personality.

She'd changed a lot in the short time they had been on this assignment together... she was less combative, more receptive. He thrilled to the knowledge that he might have had a hand in her metamorphosis.

"Are you sure you're ready for this?" he teased.

"Yes."

"Okay, but remember you asked for it."

"Knock it off with the suspense. Tell me already. What's your name?"

"My given name is Horatio Eugene."

"No!" she gasped. "Not really? Horatio Eugene?" The bed shook with her barely contained mirth.

"Ah, no laughing. You promised."

"That's truly terrible."

"Why do you think I go by Nick?"

"Poor Nicky. What was your mother thinking?"

"At least she didn't name me Sue."

"Still, Horatio Eugene!" Her giddy sigh echoed in the small room like butterfly wings against a windowpane.

"I was named after my grandfathers. I suppose Mom thought it would build character."

"What did she call you when you were a kid?"

"Gene."

"That's not so bad."

"Face a few schoolyard bullies, and you'll change your

mind. I started calling myself Nick in second grade. I think even the teachers were relieved."

"I'd never name my kid something so outrageous," Michele vowed.

"I thought you said you weren't ever getting married," Nick reminded her.

"Where have you been, Nick? Women don't have to be married to have kids."

"You'd seriously consider having a child out of wedlock?"

"I don't know." She sounded irritated. "I suppose I want children someday, but I admit I'm pretty sour on the idea of marriage."

"Yeah. I hear you, but a kid needs a father. It's a tough world out there. Children deserve every advantage."

"Guess we're both carrying a lot of baggage from our childhood," she said. "What was your father like?"

"My old man was an alcoholic. Used to beat my mom, my three brothers, and me on a daily basis."

Michele sucked in her breath. "How awful."

"You don't know the half of it."

The old memories came at him from the darkness, the whippings, the weekly appearance by the police, the sense of worthlessness he'd felt at being unable to protect his mother.

"I'm listening," Michele said softly.

Once he began dredging up the past, he couldn't seem to stop. All the old anger and pain he'd kept tamped down for so long came rolling out. He talked about the slums in South Houston where he was raised, his younger brothers, his hard-working, downtrodden mother. He talked and talked and talked until at last, depleted, he lapsed into a prolonged silence.

He'd never unburdened himself like that to anyone, not even his ex-wife, and the instinctive loosening of his guard frightened him. Why had he revealed these things to her and what must Michele think of him now?

Her small hand crept across the covers to close over his. Her touch sent a jolt of awareness straight through his heart. She genuinely cared about him! His spirits soared. Soon the case would be over, and he and Michele would go their separate ways unless he did something to change that. Could they possibly have a future together? Did he dare hope?

He refused to take advantage of Michele. When and if he made love to her, it would be because she came to him willingly with love in her heart, not because she pitied him.

Hold your horses, Nickerson; one step at a time. First, survive the night nestled in the bed next to her.

"I'm so sorry, Nick," she whispered. "I had no idea." She squeezed his hand, and for the first time in many years, he felt utterly vulnerable.

"That was a long time ago."

"And here I was whining about my privileged childhood. You probably wanted to choke me."

"Not at all. Your pain wasn't any less than mine. Just different."

"Are we a pair or what?"

"Yeah," Nick agreed. "We're a pair."

A resounding hush engulfed the room, the word pair left hanging in the air.

"We better get to sleep," he said gruffly, pulling his hand from hers and flopping onto his side. "Four o'clock comes early."

"You're right," she replied, but he could tell from her tone she was hurt.

"Good night." He wadded the pillow under his head and tried his best to ignore the sudden throbbing in his groin.

"Good night." Michele stared up at the ceiling, her throat parched, her head filled with a dozen vivid images—images of Nick. His powerful arms wrapped around her body, his delicious lips locked tightly on her mouth, his strong fingers laced through her hair.

What a man! Confidently picking the lock to Dr. Felix's office, his naughty wink including her in the process. Bravely protecting her against the vicious Rottweiler by offering his own body as sacrifice. Tenderly playing with poor little Katie, encouraging the child to laugh. Gallantly accepting responsibility for her mistakes and diverting Charboneau's displeasure.

Michele's heart caught. How could she not love him?

Nick.

He was everything she wanted, yet everything she feared. Hadn't she vowed never to fall for a commanding, authoritative guy? Hadn't being raised by a dominant, oppressive father shown her that she could never live in peace with such a man?

But the attraction was intense and undeniable. Yes, a union between her and Nick was bound to be exciting, passionate, all-encompassing. But because of that passion, a long-term relationship was doomed to burn out. It could only end in disaster, just as her parents' marriage had collapsed. Their daily clashes would intensify, the conflict building until they could no longer compromise. She had witnessed it first-hand. Two headstrong personalities in one family just would not work.

Michele lay still, listening to Nick's ragged breathing. She did not dare move. Her hands still tingled from where she'd touched him, the nerve endings alive with pleasure. Lying here beside him was such a stupid thing to do, and yet, she could not force herself to get up.

Was there any way things might work out between them?

Could they both learn to respect the other's opinion without continually having to have their own way?

Oh, how she wanted to hope!

Despite her misgivings about matrimony, in her heart, Michele was like anyone else, longing for a blissful marriage, a lovely home, healthy children.

And now it seemed she'd fallen in love with roguish Nickerson, who represented the very antithesis to those latent dreams. Marriage to him would be a constant battleground over control. They were both dedicated law enforcement officers wedded to their jobs. Not the best arrangement for raising children. Could happiness ever be hers?

Maybe she could learn to modify her behavior, to control her temper and compromise her desires. If they were willing to try...

No. A pipe dream. A young girl's silly fantasy. There was no such thing as Prince Charming and happily ever after.

But still, some part of her refused to relinquish those fanciful expectations. These last few days pretending to be married to Nick had agitated dormant feelings, tugging at her with an overwhelming wistfulness. More than anything, she wanted him to make love to her. To enter her willing body with a velvet push and claim her as his own.

Michele hissed in air through clenched teeth and pulled the cotton sheet up to her neck. If Nick ever made love to her, she would be hooked, and there would be no going back.

A cool breeze wafted in from the open window. The air smelled of hay and dew. She cast a glance over at his motionless body and wondered if Nick was asleep. Was he, too, tormented by his body's treacherous desires? Did he find rest impossible?

Maybe, Michele thought. Maybe, maybe, maybe.

After the case was over, when things had settled down,

she and Nickerson could go out on a real date and explore this "thing" between them.

Until then, she had better take care of business and find out exactly who was involved with doping the racehorses. Because the sooner they caught the culprits and ended this investigation, the sooner she and Nick would be free to explore the budding chemical reaction between them and see if it was possible to fan the sparks of their lurking passion into the blistering heat of a blazing fire.

❦

A NOISE YANKED NICK FROM A LIGHT SLEEP. IMMEDIATELY alert, he bolted to an upright position, disoriented for a moment in the unfamiliar surroundings. He looked over and saw Michele's sleeping form mounded under the covers beside him.

A sappy smile graced his face. She was still here!

It took every ounce of willpower he possessed not to lean over and trail kisses down her lovely neck. His hands ached to cup her firm buttocks; his loins cried out to consummate his desperate lust for her. How he wanted to bury his face in her red-gold hair and inhale Michele's cinnamon scent. How he longed to plant his hard body into hers and never, ever let her go.

The sound came again, a distant engine's growl, shattering his seductive thoughts. Nick cocked his head, listening.

Who could be driving around at this time of night?

He glanced at his wristwatch and saw it was just after midnight. Throwing back the covers, his feet hit the floor with a muffled thud. He felt in the darkness for his blue jeans, then tugged them up over his naked body.

Headlights slanted in through the bedroom window as

first one vehicle, then another, rumbled by the dirt road outside the cottage. Something was going down.

Nick tiptoed out of the bedroom, reluctant to wake Michele. She needed her rest, and the late-night activity might not be anything significant. Besides, if things got ugly, he didn't want her involved.

The intense feeling of protectiveness surging through his chest surprised Nick. He remembered in terrifying detail the incidents of that December night in the truck stop parking lot. The last thing he wanted was a repeat performance. She'd be angry when she woke up and found him gone, but he'd cross that bridge later.

He grinned to himself at the thought of her fierceness. She was such an independent cuss, and she hated to be left out of a good fight. But there was no sense in alarming her unnecessarily. He'd investigate and be back before she ever knew he was gone.

❧ 16 ❧

Clicking the bedroom door closed behind him, Nick walked into the living room, and searched through his duffel bag until he located his duty weapon. Pulling on a shirt, he strapped on the gun, then worked his feet into his boots.

Another vehicle rumbled by. Nick opened the front door and stepped out onto the porch in time to see the taillights of a horse trailer disappear up the hill.

Crickets chirped. Horses whinnied. The damp air felt thick and heavy. Nick stroked his jaw with a thumb and forefinger, his mind whirling at a furious pace.

Should he wake Michele? The male in him wanted her to stay curled up in bed, safe and sound, but the law enforcement officer part of him knew it was foolish to go out alone. Michele was his partner and had every right to be in on this.

He stood there a moment, frozen by indecision. If he abandoned her in solo pursuit of their quarry, she'd be furious. But if he took her along and something happened, he'd never be able to forgive himself.

When had his feelings gotten so personal?

More than anything, he wanted to protect Michele from life's ugly underbelly. He hated the idea of her being a DPS officer. It was dirty work, and she deserved better. Like his mother had deserved a man who cherished and loved her, not the drunken tyrant she'd married.

Driven by his need to shelter Michele, no matter the cost, Nick made his choice. He'd go without her. If his action destroyed their budding trust, then so be it; he'd rather have her mad and healthy than injured or even killed.

Satisfied with his initial decision to leave her sleeping, Nick traversed the hill behind the cottage. A rising half-moon provided him with a modicum of light, but the darkened pasture loomed like an unknown minefield.

He crested the rise and peered down into the valley below. Long grass whispered in the breeze, shimmering like fish scales. A quarter mile in the distance, he spotted a circle of headlights.

This is probably nothing, he thought. But he patted his holstered gun for reassurance. He had a nagging feeling that something wasn't right.

Nick trod through the pasture, his thoughts on Michele. She stirred hopeful feelings within him, feelings of love, family, commitment. Since the collapse of his marriage to Julianna, Nick had convinced himself he was not the marrying kind, but Michele Mallory had him believing anything was possible.

Once the investigation was over, perhaps they could explore their burgeoning attraction. It had been so hard, lying in bed next to her, unable to kiss her, squeeze her, hold her close.

Charboneau would have your hide if he knew what you were thinking, Nickerson.

Skirting a dump of oak trees, Nick smiled to himself. That would teach the lieutenant to put two headstrong control freaks of the opposite gender on assignment together.

What would Charboneau think if he and Michele got married?

Married.

The word lingered in his mind like an echo. Married to Michele for real? Not like this pretend marriage they'd been living for the past few days, but a real marriage where each night was consummated by wondrous lovemaking.

Unconsciously, Nick fingered the ring on his left hand and realized he wanted Michele Mallory as his bride. Desperately, hungrily, immediately. He wanted this case solved. Now. He wanted to be free to court Michele, see where this crazy chemistry took them.

The cloud bank slid over the moon, dashing Nick in darkness. Only the light from the vehicle headlamps shining two hundred yards in the distance guided his way. He could barely make out the perimeters of a neglected bush track.

A boisterous guffaw rang out, followed by a horse's neighing. Voices, mostly male but one female, reached Nick's ears.

What were they up to? Did they bring the horses here to dope them? Were they exchanging drugs for cash? Nick wondered, dragging a hand along his jaw.

Crouching down, he inched closer.

He saw people walking around, horses in tow, the headlights cutting a swath across the bush track. A woman's giggle filled the air.

Elvira.

Nick clenched his teeth. Damn. He hated that the perky little jockey was involved in this.

He saw Steve Bradshaw and a couple of other ranch hands. He cocked his head, listening.

This was it. An arrest in the doping was imminent.

And Michele wasn't here to share the moment.

Sudden guilt stabbed through him. He shouldn't have left her sleeping. This was Michele's bust, too. She should be here fighting beside him. They were a team, after all.

For once, he regretted his own bid for control. By taking charge of the situation, he'd left Michele out entirely.

As he sat crouching in the long grass, he watched Elvira swing up on the back of one horse, while a person he didn't know mounted another horse and headed for the bush track.

He waited, indecision growing with the tension. Should he go and get Michele? What if the cowboys left before he got back? Perhaps he should go down alone and arrest everyone? What if they were armed?

Damn. Why had he acted like such a stupid Neanderthal, thinking he could handle this without Michele? Hadn't he learned anything from his short-lived marriage? Hadn't he realized it required give and take to make a relationship work? He was thirty-four years old and still behaving like that desperate fifteen-year-old trying hard to prove he was a man.

Observing Elvira and the other rider lining up at the bush track gate, it finally dawned on Nick what was happening in the valley below. This wasn't a drug deal at all. He'd merely stumbled across a match race.

As that revelation set in, Nick suddenly felt reborn. Michele would never have to know he'd betrayed her as his partner. He'd leave the cowboys to their illegal gambling and hurry back to the cottage. He had something vital to tell Michele Mallory. Something that could change both their lives.

"Nick?"

Michele reached over in the bed next to her. Empty. Swinging her feet over the edge, she reached for the light switch, bathing the room in a pale glow. She glanced at the clock. Fifteen minutes before one.

"Nick?" she called again, padding to the door. If he was in the bathroom, she didn't want to disturb him.

She stepped into the hallway. The rest of the cottage lay in darkness.

"Nick?" she repeated, moving through the little house, turning on lamps as she went.

In the living room, she spotted his unzipped duffel bag gaping open on the couch.

A knot of suspicion rose in her mind. Grabbing his duffel, she turned it upside down on the hardwood floor. Out rolled socks, T-shirts, blue jeans, and an empty ammunition box.

No gun. No bullets.

The absence of his duty weapon told the unvarnished truth. Nickerson had slipped away in the night to go investigating on his own.

The knowledge struck her like an open palm across the face.

How could he sneak off without her? Especially after the closeness that they'd shared in that queen-size bed. Apparently, she'd been wrong to think the histories they'd shared had drawn them nearer to each other. What a fool she'd been to believe his confidence meant the feelings they had for each other could develop into something special! How could she love a man she didn't trust?

But she did love him.

No. Michele set her jaw. She wouldn't, couldn't love a man who didn't have enough respect for her identity as a law enforcement officer to include her in his plans. How dare he! They were on this case together. They were supposed to be a team.

Storming back into the bedroom, she shucked off her

sleep shirt and got dressed. When she found Horatio Eugene Nickerson, there would be hell to pay.

He had changed the rules of their relationship, and she found that betrayal intolerable. He'd poured out his heart to her in the blackness of the bedroom, giving her the impression that she mattered to him, then doing something so unforgivable as sneaking off without her.

It's for your own good, Michele. Her father's voice echoed in her head. *To protect you from yourself.*

Judge Mallory had uttered those cruel words when she'd discovered he'd paid off her first real boyfriend, telling her the boy was no good, that he had only been dating her for her money. The fact that her father was right just made things more painful.

Her father had continuously tried to control her life. Even now, the memory seared her mind. Yes. Nickerson was just like her father. How could she ever have thought to trust him?

She felt like a blindsided fool. How could she have been so gullible?

Strapping on her duty weapon and shoving a canister of pepper spray in her pocket, Michele turned off all the lights and eased out of the cottage, every instinct at full alert.

The night air was cool. She paused for a moment on the porch, allowing her eyes to adjust to the dark.

Where could Nick have gone?

Logic told her the stables. She saw her pickup looming in the driveway. So he'd disappeared on foot.

An owl hooted from a cottonwood tree, causing Michele to clutch for the gun holstered at her shoulder. Sheepishly, she lowered her arm.

What was Nick up to? Had he waited patiently for her to fall asleep, then slipped out of bed to search Hollis's office again?

A mockingbird trilled, but she heard nothing else. The smell of hay, sawdust, horses, and roses drifted on the breeze. A few fireflies flickered through the underbrush.

Everything was quiet. Too quiet. Unexpectedly, she shivered, and goosebumps carpeted her arms.

A furtive movement caught her eye. Someone was out there. In the darkness. She ducked behind a bush, her pulse thudding. Drawing her duty weapon, she crouched, waiting, breath bated.

The grass rustled. Michele peered around the bush, studying the approaching figure in the wan moonlight.

His cocky swagger gave him away. She'd know that arrogant walk anywhere.

She sprang up in front of him.

Nick shied, startled, taking a step backward, and he raised a hand to his chest.

"Where the hell have you been?" she demanded.

"Damn, Michele, you scared the life out of me."

"What do you mean sneaking off in the dark without me?"

"You want to aim somewhere else?" He waved at the 9mm Beretta clutched in her hands.

She hesitated a moment before holstering her gun. "What exactly are you trying to pull, Nick?" Anger mixed with desire as her gaze swept his tall, imposing body. Why did he have to excite her so? Even now, at the height of her anger, she wanted him.

No. She'd already let passion make a fool of her once, she wasn't about to fall for his nefarious charms again.

"Just going for a walk, babe."

Don't lie to me and don't you dare call me 'babe'."

"Calm down. What's wrong?"

"I can't trust you."

"Ah, Michele, what are you talking about?" But he

couldn't hide the truth from her, the sheepish look on his face told the tale.

"You took your gun with you. You went investigating on your own, without me. Admit it."

"Michele..." He extended his arm and took a step toward her.

She raised both palms. "Don't even think about touching me."

"Stop being irrational."

"Don't tell me what to do, Nick." She vehemently shook her head.

"I'm trying not to get angry with you." He spoke through clenched teeth.

"Excuse me, but I'm the one entitled to get angry." Temper flaring hot as a pancake griddle, she stepped forward and thrust out her chin. "I know exactly what you did."

"What are you talking about?" He stood ramrod stiff, not backing off an inch.

"You went investigating on your own to protect me, didn't you? I'm the poor, frail female partner, and you're the big, tough man in control. That's it, isn't it?"

"Michele, you're shouting."

"I've got every reason to shout. Remember what happened that night Harbarger shot me? I fell asleep in the patrol car, and you slipped off to do some snooping without me."

"You weren't supposed to wake up," he said.

"Just like tonight."

"Listen, I made a mistake."

"Darn right you did."

"I hate that you got shot," his voice was husky, "but if you'd just stayed in the car like I told you, it wouldn't have happened."

"There you go again. Deciding what's best for me." She tossed her head and met his cold glare.

Nick's black eyes glistened steely, uncompromising. Moonlight glinted off the thin scar riding his jaw, hard-edged and menacing. Michele understood why felons feared him.

"I came back for you," he said. The wind gusted, tossing his dark curls about his collar.

"Why?"

Dear Lord, he looked so damned sexy. She wanted to release her anger and throw herself into his strong arms, but how could she? If she allowed him to control her life and the investigation, he would take her acquiescence as a sign that she welcomed his dominion.

"I was wrong to leave you out of the investigation," he said.

"You expect me to believe you?"

❦

HE SHRUGGED NONCHALANTLY, BUT THE CHAOTIC emotions surging through his chest were anything but casual. He wanted her, needed her, and yet, he seemed to anger her at every turn.

"If we're ever going to have a relationship, Michele, we've got to learn to trust each other."

"How can I trust a man who slips out on me in the middle of the night? Not once, but twice."

"Look, I just wanted to protect you. Is that so wrong?" Nick raised his palms in a defensive gesture. Didn't she understand that he felt obligated to shield the people he loved? Couldn't she see he offered his protection as a precious gift, not as a cage to contain her spirit?

"You sound exactly like my father!" Michele fumed. "I'm a

grown woman, and I don't need a stand-in daddy running interference."

"I messed up. Okay? How many times do I have to apologize?"

"You don't get it, do you? Apologies are useless, Nick. It's your whole mindset. You'll never change. I doubt you can." The clouds moved and shifted overhead, hiding the moon, eclipsing her face.

"I'm not your father," he said harshly. "Don't try to warp me into that mold. I don't want to control your life."

"Oh, no?" She took another step forward and tilted her face up to his. They were toe-to-toe. "Then why do you keep making choices for me?"

Because I love you.

The words badgered Nick's mind, but he clamped his lips together to prevent himself from uttering them out loud. The stark reality scared him. Michele Mallory had gotten under his skin. He realized just how much he was going to miss her pugnacious attitude when this case was over.

"Come on, Michele, admit it. Despite all your denial to the contrary, you're attracted to my strength, my self-confidence. You like me to take charge. It's exciting."

"Nick, you are the most arrogant, egotistical, son of a... gun I've ever had the misfortune to meet."

He wanted to grasp her by the shoulders and shake her. Instead, he gritted his teeth and folded his hands into fists. Did the woman ever retreat? He unclenched a fist and ran his hand along her bare arm.

"Tell me I don't stimulate you." He goaded her because he didn't want her to know the truth—the idea of her spurning his love was too unbearable to conceive.

She shook her arm free. "You're a jerk." But she didn't move, staying right in the line of fire.

Passion swept him, hot and powerful. Her ire excited him.

He wanted her. Here, now, on the soft ground. He wanted to hear her moan his name, see her face contort with ecstasy as he made love to her.

Nick leaned his head down, the heady scent of her filling his nostrils. Glory, she looked sexy when she was mad, with that pout on her peachy mouth, those navy eyes gleaming with energy.

Without another word, he took control. Wrapping one arm around her waist, he pulled her tight against his chest.

Her breath came in short, shallow gasps. "Don't you dare kiss me, Nick."

"No?"

"I'm serious. You kiss me again, and I'm telling Charboneau you've compromised the investigation."

"Why? Are you afraid my kisses will drive you wild?"

"In your dreams."

"And yours."

Heaven help her, he was right! She did want his kiss! Could almost taste him against her tongue. But how could she surrender herself to a man she couldn't trust? A man who refused to see her as an equal? A man who would thwart her at every turn as her father had done her mother?

He nestled his cheek against hers. She savored the feel of his scratchy beard against her soft skin. There was no denying he was all man. Tough and masculine. Cocky and self-assured.

How could she be so attracted to the very qualities that represented everything she resisted in a man? Perhaps that was why she'd never had a serious relationship before. She could not reconcile the duality of her feelings.

His lips tumbled down on hers with the intensity of an imploding building.

She absorbed the shock of his tongue against her teeth. Murmured deep in her throat. No. She couldn't allow him to thwart her in this manner. She had good reason to be angry, and she refused to let him sidetrack her. Michele had to do something. Had to stop this kiss before she was whisked away by her baser urges.

Placing her hands against his chest, she pushed him away. "No, Nick. We cannot do this."

"Why is it so hard for us, Michele?" Nick asked, sounding all the world like a confused child.

"I don't know," she whispered, flooded with a storm of conflicting sensations as he released her from his grip and stepped away.

"I'm going back to the cottage," he said. "Are you coming?"

"No."

"Suit yourself."

"Wait a minute." Michele touched his shoulder and immediately regretted it as warm spirals of desire drifted from him to her. "I'm your partner. I have a right to know what you were doing out there."

"Nothing worth blowing our cover over."

"See! There you go again. Keeping things from me. Just like you did that night at the truck stop."

"Don't get all excited, Michele. Steve Bradshaw, Elvira Montrose, and a few others are having a match race on a bush track at the back of the ranch. Happy now?"

"How do you know that's all they're doing? Come on, we've got to get over there."

"I said there's no need."

"And I want to draw that conclusion for myself, thank you very much."

"Then go."

"I will."

"Fine." Nick turned on his heels and started stalking back to the cottage.

"Fine, then. I'm taking Jet."

"What?" Nick stopped in his tracks, whirling around to

face her. The moon continued to play peekaboo with the clouds, darting in and out, bathing the ground first in light and then in blackness. "You're not taking that stallion out alone in the dark. I forbid it."

"Excuse me?" Michele settled her hands on her hips. "I don't believe you have a choice."

"As senior officer here, I am in charge. If you're injured, you will compromise the investigation."

"You're acting foolish. I'll be perfectly safe on Jet."

"You are not going." He stormed over to her, his eyes snapping fire. "Do you understand."

"Unless you bodily restrain me, yes, I am."

"Don't tempt me, woman."

"Don't tell me what to do, man."

"Go on, then." He waved an arm.

She stood there a moment, staring at him. "You're not going to try and stop me?"

"What would be the use? If you're determined to have things your own way, even to the detriment of your health, there's nothing I can do about it."

And with that he stalked away, leaving her alone in the darkness.

Michele should never have allowed herself to hope that things between her and Nickerson could ever work out. They were completely wrong for each other. They fought like lions and tigers.

And kissed liked they were in love.

She watched him disappear into the cottage, then she resolutely headed for the stables. More than investigating the match race, she only wanted to ride, to clear her head and attempt to make some sense of her jumbled emotions.

But how? Nickerson had embedded himself in her mind, forever changing the way she viewed the world. Before going undercover with him, she'd been so sure of what she wanted in life—a successful career, independence, the respect of her peers. But suddenly that wasn't enough. She longed for much more.

She'd dared to dream of something she'd always yearned for but never had.

A real family.

With a mother and father who cherished each other and worked in tandem to raise healthy, loving children. Not pulling at opposing poles like her parents, who had created a child leery of relationships, scared to fall in love.

Stop it, Michele. Forget about Nickerson.

Yeah, right. Might as well forget about the sun and the moon and the stars.

Slipping through the shadows, Michele walked past the bunkhouse, headed for the stables and Jet. She was surprised to see Dr. Felix's truck parked in the yard. Was a horse sick?

A light shining in the window of Jim Hollis's office caught her attention. What was going on?

Michele pressed her body against the corrugated tin building that housed the offices at one end, tack room and stables at the other.

A horse nickered in the distance. The moist earth shifted beneath her booted feet.

Closer and closer she inched until she was standing just under and to the right of the open window. She heard murmured voices. Taking yet another step, she tilted her head and strained her ears, struggling to identify the speakers.

"Don't be stupid," a man hissed. "There's no turning back."

Michele frowned. The voice was familiar.

"They're onto us." The other voice sounded nervous. Jim Hollis?

"They have no proof."

"All the more reason we should stop now!" The man raised his voice. It *was* Jim Hollis.

"You don't get it, Hollis. We have to go through with this. Too much is riding on the outcome."

"You tell Mario I'm finished turning a blind eye."

"You forget, my friend, you could be exposed at any time. Then where would you and your precious granddaughter be?"

Michele still couldn't identify the other voice. But she knew it. Gnawing her lip, she tried frantically to rack her brain.

"Don't you dare threaten Katie!" Jim sounded deadly.

"Do as I say, and there'll be no need for threats."

Panic skittered through Michele. She grabbed for her duty weapon, withdrew it from the holster, and marshaled the gun in both hands. She stood with her back pressed against the building, the coolness of the metal seeping through her cotton T-shirt.

What should she do? Burst in? Announce they were under arrest? But what evidence did she have, other than what she had overheard? Hearsay wouldn't hold up in a court of law. She found herself wishing Nick were here.

Hollis sighed the thick, heavy sigh of a man recognizing defeat. "All right, but Jet is absolutely the last one."

Jet! They were planning to dope the beautiful stallion? No!

In that second, Michele knew what she had to do first. Get Jet out of his stall and to safety. Then she could decide how to proceed.

Her heart pounding like a hammer against her rib cage, Michele dashed to the stables. Holstering her gun, she fumbled with the door latch, wrenching it open at last. The horses shifted in their stalls, some greeting Michele with low whinnies.

"Shhh," Michele cautioned uselessly. She must locate Jet

and get him out of there before Hollis and the unknown man discovered her.

Jet's stall was situated at the rear of the stables, far from the office but almost as far from the door.

Where was Nick when she needed him? Dammit, she could have used his help. That's what happened when one member of the team went off like a maverick.

Like that night you tried to arrest Harbarger alone?

Remorse zinged through Michele as she crept past the other horses. Sawdust and hay muffled her footsteps. She should never have turned Nick in to Internal Affairs. After all, she had disobeyed his orders. Just thinking about that night had her old gunshot wound aching.

Nickerson made her feel so conflicted. One minute she wanted nothing more to do with the man, the next she longed desperately to dissolve into the warm circle of his arms.

"No time for this, Michele," she said out loud. "They're coming to dope Jet."

Feeling her way in the darkness, she found the stallion's stall at last.

Jet nickered a greeting.

Grabbing the bridle hanging from the peg outside the stall gate, Michele cooed to the horse and scratched the knob at the top of his head. She slipped the bridle in place, swung open the door and guided Jet out into the stables, her ears acutely attuned for sounds of intruders.

Jet balked, digging his hooves into the sawdust floor.

Michele clicked her tongue. She stroked the stallion's muzzle, urging him forward.

"Come on, fella," she coaxed. "It's just you and me. Let's go for a midnight ride."

The horse pricked up his ears and swished his tail.

"That's a good boy." Michele swallowed back her panic. She couldn't allow Jet to sense her anxiety.

A door slammed. Footsteps sounded in the distance.

They were coming!

Alarmed, Michele tugged harder on Jet's bridle, urging him toward the open door.

The stallion lifted his head. Something in the field outside had caught his interest. Probably the scent of a mare. Without further enticement, Jet bolted for the door, dragging Michele along with him.

"Whoa," she whispered, trying hard to control the randy beast. "At least let me get on your back before we take off."

There would be no time for a saddle, Michele realized and gulped. She'd have to vault aboard.

Then what?

No matter how she might wish otherwise, she needed help. The answer floated through her mind, clear and sensible.

Get Nick.

HANDS CLASPED BEHIND HIS BACK, NICK PACED THE SMALL cottage.

Dammit, he shouldn't have let Michele go off on her own. He should have forced her to come back to the house with him.

How?

That was the two-edged sword she wielded over him. She perceived his desire to protect her as a need to control, and that wasn't how he saw things at all. If he hoped to win her heart, he had no choice but to back off.

But it was so hard not marching out there, dragging her

off the horse kicking and screaming if he had to, for her own safety.

Unexpectedly, Nick remembered the advice Charboneau had given him about dealing with Michele

Let her make her own mistakes, the lieutenant had said. *She'll appreciate you for it.*

"I'm trying, Lieutenant, I'm trying," Nick mumbled under his breath. "But how do I shake this nagging dread?"

And he did feel uneasy.

Anxiety squirmed in his stomach like a basketful of snakes. The hairs on the back of his neck stuck out straight. He couldn't stop pacing, and he felt as if the walls of the cottage were getting smaller and smaller. Something terrible was going to happen to Michele.

He felt it.

What if he went after her and nothing was wrong?

Michele would verbally chew a hole in the seat of his pants.

Not that he shied away from the sharp side of her tongue. Nick grinned to himself. Truth be known, he liked the sparks they created when they were scrapping. What Nick feared was turning Michele away from him for good.

He had to prove he was different from her father.

But she had gone riding a wild stallion in the middle of the night. It was dangerous and stupid.

And he'd driven her to it.

Nick grimaced as the memory of Michele's gunshot wound floated through his mind. That had been his fault as well. She shouldn't be out there alone with untamed stallions and criminals bent on doping racehorses for profit.

His heart fisted.

He had to go after her. Even if it meant risking any chance for romance.

Nick stormed from the cottage, rehearsing his speech. He

was going to approach her sensibly. He wasn't going to tell her what to do, merely point out that riding at two in the morning was not a good idea.

Gravel crunched under his boots as he walked down the path to the stables. He wondered if the match race was over and where the ranch hands had gone.

He reached the stables in five minutes, every sense at full alert. His ears strained to hear past the usual night noises, his eyes searching the shadowy ranch.

Nick spotted the light at the headquarters building, heard the restless nickering of horses in their stalls. The dry, earthy scent of hay and sawdust lingered in the air.

Where was Michele? He stopped and ran a hand along his day's growth of beard, pondering what to do next.

He'd known she would react this way. So why had he left her sleeping?

Because you're a macho jerk, and you're going to lose her if you don't change your ways, Nickerson.

More lights came on in the stables. Curious, Nick cocked his head and listened. The sound of angry voices floated out to him. Arguing.

Was Michele in the stables fighting with someone?

Determined, Nick stalked toward the building, throwing caution to the wind. Just as he reached the stable door, a horse loomed out of the blackness. Jet.

Startled, Nick took a step back and raised his arm.

The stallion let out a high-pitched cry and vaulted over the fence. That's when Nick realized there was someone aboard, flattened low against the horse's back.

"Michele!" he shouted as the Thoroughbred raced through the field and disappeared into the night. "Come back!"

But just as he wondered how to pursue her, the stable

doors flew open, distributing a shaft of light through the darkness. Two figures stood in the doorway.

Instinctively, Nick drew his duty weapon. "Hands up!" he commanded. He realized he'd just blown their cover, but something told him this was the confrontation he'd been sent here to resolve.

Stalking closer, Nick narrowed his eyes as he identified the men holding their arms aloft.

Jim Hollis and Dr. Richard Felix.

"Well, well, well," Nick drawled, low and deadly, his gun trained on them. "What have we here?"

"Excuse me," Dr. Felix said in his pompous manner. "What right do you have drawing a gun on us?" The vet tilted his aquiline nose at a haughty angle.

"I want to know exactly what's going on here." Nick kept his gaze firmly focused on the pair. He didn't trust them. Not for a minute.

"Jim called me. The stallion was sick," Dr. Felix said. He shot Hollis a warning glance.

Nick shifted his gaze from the vet to the trainer. "Jim? Are you sticking by his story?"

"Who *are* you?" Hollis asked. Nick saw the man was trembling.

"Sergeant Nick Nickerson with the Department of Public Safety."

Hollis looked from Nick to Felix and back again. "It's over, Richard."

"Don't you dare say a damn word, Hollis, or you're a dead man."

"I've had it. I can't turn a blind eye any longer while you dope horses." Hollis lowered his arms and turned to face the vet.

"Hands up, Jimbo," Nick motioned with his gun.

"Look, Nickerson." Hollis inched his hands back over his head. "I'm ready to give myself up. I want to talk."

"Shut up," Felix screamed. "Who do you think is going to pay for your granddaughter's transplant if you spill your guts?"

"Katie's on her way to get a liver as we speak," Hollis crowed triumphantly. "Jenna called me an hour ago. That's where I was headed when you showed up."

"You won't get away with it," Felix threatened.

"The money Mario paid me has already been given to the hospital. There's no getting it back. That's why I wanted out. I only participated in the first place because of Katie. I'm turning myself in to Nickerson here." Hollis jerked his head at Nick.

"Mario'll get you for this," Felix hissed.

"I don't think so," Nick said. "You fellas are under arrest for manufacturing illegal amphetamines and administering them to racehorses."

"Go ahead," the veterinarian crowed. "Arrest us. You have no proof. We'll walk before dawn. It's my word against Hollis's."

Nick grimaced. Felix was right.

"Search his bag," Hollis said, nervously shaking a hand. "He injected Jet with the newest strain of the drug about twenty minutes ago. He wanted to test it out before the races this weekend."

"Traitor!" Felix shouted.

Nick waved the gun at the vet. "Be quiet!" He turned his attention to Hollis. "What did you just say?"

"Felix injected the stallion..."

Nick's heart flopped sickeningly as the implication of the trainer's words smacked him.

Michele was riding a wild stallion injected with a high-powered amphetamine. Alone. In the dark.

She was in danger again, and it was all his fault. Both

times he'd sought to protect her, he had instead placed her in deeper jeopardy.

Dear Lord, he had to get her off that horse before she was killed! But what about Felix and Hollis? His mind whirled, racing at a furious pace. What to do?

Suddenly, Felix lunged for Hollis, deciding the issue.

"I'm not going down because of you," the veterinarian cried, wrapping his hands around Hollis's neck.

"Hold it," Nick demanded, sounding to his own ears like John Wayne on a rampage. "Don't make me use this." He waved his duty weapon at the two struggling men. "My wife is out there riding a hopped-up horse, and I've got to find her. It would make things a lot easier for me if I just shot you both."

❧ 18 ❧

Something was wrong with Jet.

His large body was tense, his sides heaving as he breathed. He frantically wrung his tail, and his heart thundered so fast Michele felt the vibrations through her thighs.

The stallion galloped across the ebony fields, Michele clinging to his back like a skydiver to a parachute.

She tried to slow him, pulling back sharply on the reins, but Jet ignored her command, merely threw back his head, and whinnied, the very skin on his body twitching.

"Whoa, boy. Whoa." She kneed him in the flank. That signal, too, was disobeyed.

If anything, Jet picked up speed, his hooves rumbling across the earth, his glossy body hurling through space.

Michele bumped and jostled, her teeth clacking together with each jarring step.

Could Dr. Felix have already doped Jet, she wondered, fear's icy fingers snatching at her throat. Was the stallion under the influence of dangerous drugs?

Michele shuddered. It would explain the animal's bizarre behavior.

Why hadn't she listened to Nick? He'd told her not to ride Jet.

No. He had ordered her not to ride him. That's why she'd foolishly gone to the stables. Her hardheaded, stubborn desire to prove herself had landed Michele in this compromising position, just like that night at the truck stop.

Oh, if she could turn back the clock.

But hindsight was twenty-twenty. Right now, she had more profound problems. Like how to get off Jet's back without getting herself killed.

She tried again to rein him in, but Jet shook his head so violently, the leather snapped beneath her fingers, and Michele's arm flailed wildly. Terrified, she dropped the useless reins and laced her fingers through the stallion's mane and prayed.

Jet flew like hell demons breathed fire on his heels.

Michele squeezed her eyes tightly shut. How long before the drug wore off and Jet wound down? He couldn't sustain this pace forever.

The night enveloped them, tight as a glove. She slipped on his back and cried out. Her eyes opened wide in time to see him headed for a thicket of oak trees.

"No, Jet, no," she screamed.

But the horse paid no heed.

Clutching and grasping, she tried her best to remain astride the massive beast. Tree branches whooshed by, scratching at her pant legs. She'd known someone once who'd been run under a tree branch and killed.

Michele could see the same fate befalling her. She had to get off the horse. Now.

But how?

Jet broke through the thicket and started down a slight incline into a grass field. Beyond that loomed a virtual forest.

It's now or never, Mallory.

Looking down at the ground rushing beneath her, Michele swallowed hard. Could she dismount?

She must! She stood a far better chance of surviving if she initiated the fall.

Jet seemed to slow slightly.

She saw the opportunity and took it.

Sucking in a deep breath, Michele closed her eyes, let go, and rolled off the stallion's back.

ॐ

AS QUICKLY AS HE COULD, NICK TIED HOLLIS AND FELIX with nylon rope, then locked Hollis in his office closet and Felix in the tack room. Each minute not knowing where Michele was burned like an agonizing hour in his craw.

If she was seriously hurt, he'd give up law enforcement forever. And if she was killed—

No, he couldn't think like that. Michele would be fine. But the memory of Whirlwind's outrage came back to haunt him, stark and real. If Jet acted like Whirlwind had, Nick doubted even an expert horsewoman could survive.

Stepping out of the barn, he stood in the exercise yard, bewildered. Where to start looking?

As if in cosmic answer to his question, Jet came galloping around the stables.

Riderless.

Nick's heart contracted, his stomach lurched. He felt sick. *Oh my God, please let Michele be all right.* He had to find her. Now!

But the truck was back at the cottage, and he couldn't ride well enough to search for her on horseback.

Spying Felix's truck parked in the yard, Nick sucked in a breath and prayed. He wrenched open the door.

Keys dangling from the ignition greeted him.

He rushed back to throw wide the gate, then got in the veterinarian's pickup and started off across the pasture.

"Hang on, Michele; I'm coming, babe," he said.

A weird sensation of deja vu shivered over him. He'd been in this position before, frantically searching for her, guilt consuming his every thought. Would he never learn?

She'd told him herself, but he'd been too wrapped up in being right to pay attention to her needs.

His basic urge in life was to serve and protect. It was the reason he made such a good law enforcement officer. What he tended to forget was that others didn't always welcome his intervention.

In fact, Nick now realized, Michele probably saw his impulse to take care of her as a desire to control her. Although nothing was further from the truth, Nick might see how she could assume such a thing, given her years spent bucking a dominating father. Why had it taken him so long to come to that conclusion?

The truck headlights shone through the night. He drove in the direction from which Jet had come. Could he ever convince Michele that he wasn't like her father? That even though they engaged in heated arguments, they could still have a healthy, satisfying relationship?

"Ah, give it up, Nickerson. It'll never work," he mumbled under his breath, his eyes sweeping the landscape. "Just find her, make sure she's safe, wrap up the investigation, and go back to Austin."

Oh! What a lonely thought. Back to his crummy apartment and TV dinners. Back to silence and dust balls. Back to long nights in an empty bed.

His former existence sounded so unappealing. Damn

Michele Mallory. She changed his whole perspective. Changed him!

After his divorce, before Michele, Nick had vowed to remain a bachelor. But the woman had him thinking of kids, dogs, horses, and a house with a white picket fence. Everything he'd always denied he wanted.

When his ex had left him, Nick had convinced himself he wasn't cut out for marriage. And he'd been happy playing the role of a carefree bachelor.

Until now.

"Michele, where are you?" he cried out, his heart aching, his hands gripping the steering wheel like a lifeline.

Then, as if in answer to his prayers, he saw something moving in his peripheral vision. Nick trod on the brakes. Felix's truck fishtailed to a stop.

Michele!

Throwing the vehicle into Park, Nick was out the door with the motor still running.

She hobbled toward him.

Michele was hurt!

His heart sank like the slowest horse at the Derby. His fears had come true! She'd been injured again, and it was all his fault. He had not protected her.

He dashed across the field to meet her. "Oh, babe," he said in a choked whisper. "Are you okay?"

"Jet was drugged," she said, her own voice husky.

"I know... I..." God, how he wanted to touch her, kiss her, run his fingers through her hair. But he was afraid. Would she reject him?

"I had to dive off. I think I sprained my ankle."

"Oh, Michele, I was worried sick."

"Were you?" She gave him a curious glance.

"You don't know how much."

She said nothing.

"I busted Hollis and Felix. They're the ones doing the doping. Or at least Felix was. Hollis was turning a blind eye for the money from Martuchi. Hollis confessed."

"You arrested them without me?" She sank her hands on her hips.

"Well, babe, you were off on Jet, having your temper tantrum."

"You big dufus, I wasn't having a temper tantrum. I knew it was Hollis and Felix. I heard them too. I thought they were about to drug Jet, so I was rescuing him. Too late, I found out they'd already slipped him the amphetamines."

"At least you're safe, and the culprits are securely tied and locked up."

"And you did it all without me. Just like with Harbarger."

"What was my alternative, Michele? Let them destroy the evidence while I came to look for you?"

"I don't believe your audacity, Nickerson."

Was it his imagination or did her bottom lip tremble? Was she fighting back the tears? Michele Mallory? The bravest woman he'd ever met?

Tentative orange fingers clutched the eastern sky as the morning sun struggled to make its debut. The damp grass brushed against the tops of his boots. A meadowlark sang in the distance.

"It doesn't really matter who made the arrest, just so long as it's done."

"Easy for you to say," she replied bitterly. "You're the one in control."

"We're a team, you and me. Like a saddle and blanket, working together."

"Please, Nickerson, don't patronize me. You're one hundred percent maverick, and you love it. Nobody's ever going to tame you."

"Is that what worries you, Michele, that I couldn't be a

one-woman man?" Much as he liked to flirt, Nick possessed a monogamous streak a mile wide. He'd always longed to find the right woman and build the kind of strong family structure that had been missing from his own childhood. And that woman was Michele Mallory. His heart shouted it to his brain. His gut agreed. He loved her.

"Don't even flatter yourself, Nickerson. Who would ever consider you husband material?"

"Ah, Mish." He reached out a hand to her, but she stumbled away from him. "What's the matter? Why are you feeling this way?"

"Why? Because once again, you've beaten me to the punch, Nickerson. You've made me look bad."

He shook his head. "No. That's not true. Something else is bothering you." The startled look in those navy-blue eyes told him he'd struck the truth. She was using her anger to hide her real emotions.

"Don't be ridiculous," she said, limping in the direction of Felix's truck. "Let's get back to the ranch house and get this over with."

"Let me carry you."

"No way!" she snarled at him.

"Why not?" he asked, walking beside her.

"I don't need you."

"Yes, you do."

"That's your ego talking, Nickerson."

"You're lying, babe. You need me so badly, you can taste it."

"Ha!"

"Admit the truth, Mallory. You've picked a fight with me because you can't handle me getting close to you."

"Absolutely not."

"You're afraid of relationships. That's why you've never been married, why you claim you never will get married."

"That's a lie." She stopped to glare at him.

"You're terrified of ending up in a bad relationship like your parents. You're frightened of losing your identity. That's why you won't let me get near you."

"What a load of horse dung."

He shook his head, pain piercing his chest. He hated hurting her, but he had to make her see reality if they had any hope of a future together. "I thought you were brave and strong and courageous, but you're not. It's all bluster, isn't it, Mish, to hide your fear. You're terrified of falling in love with me. You're a coward. Admit it."

Her jaw tightened. Turning, she hobbled toward the pickup once again.

"Michele?"

"I HAVE NOTHING MORE TO SAY TO YOU, NICKERSON. NOW take me back to the ranch."

True. All true. Every word Nickerson had spoken. She was terrified of falling in love with him.

Throughout the crush of activity that followed, Michele tried to stop thinking about his accusation but couldn't. Was she already in love with this rugged, masculine, authoritative man? Where had she slipped up? How could she have lowered her guard so wholly?

Stupid. Stupid. Stupid.

Back at the ranch house, they called Charboneau. After dispatching a patrol car to pick up the culprits, the lieutenant regaled them with good news of his own. The other DPS team that had been keeping Mario Martuchi under surveillance had made an arrest that night as well, catching the mobster red-handed leaving the amphetamine lab with the drugs in his possession. The case had been successfully resolved. They could all go home.

The curious ranch hands gathered on the scene, rubbing their eyes and staring in amazement as Nick rounded up Hollis and Felix for the DPS troopers.

Nick called out to Elvira, asking her to take Michele to the bunkhouse and put an ice pack on her swollen ankle.

Michele, too tired and defeated to protest, allowed Elvira to help her across the exercise yard. She rested a hand against the little jockey's shoulder, grateful for the support.

"What happened?" Elvira asked, her eyes wide. She kept darting glances over her shoulder at Nick.

"Long story." Michele waved a hand. "I'll tell you about it later."

"What's wrong with Nick?" Elvira asked. "He looks like he just lost his best friend."

Did he? As they reached the bunkhouse, Michele stopped at the porch to search the gathering crowd for a glimpse of Nick. She spotted him, head and shoulders above the rest. Her eyes soaked up the sight of him like a race-weary Thoroughbred drinking at his water trough.

Nick did look tense, his jaw thrust forward, a scowl creasing his forehead as he led a handcuffed Felix out of the stables. Michele's heart snagged in her throat. Nick was angry. At her.

Was she so wrong to resist him? Could she relinquish her need for control to explore a relationship with Nick? Could she trust him? More to the point, could she trust herself?

Oh, how she wanted more from him. But she was afraid. Petrified to surrender herself to the mind, body, and soul possession that loving Nick Nickerson would demand. It was much safer to let the feelings between them disappear, along with the conclusion of this undercover case.

"Michele." Elvira held open the screen door and studied Michele's face intently. "Are you all right?"

Swallowing past the sadness choking her throat, Michele nodded and limped into the bunkhouse.

Yes, it was smarter to ignore the emotions Nick stirred in her. Far better to let those embers die than to fan the flames and watch helplessly as passion burned to spent ashes. No relationship could sustain the intense fires that dwelled in both their psyches. Any alliance between her and Nick would be just like her parents' union, hot, spicy, and destined for failure.

"Did you and your husband have a fight?" Elvira asked, guiding Michele over to a straight-backed kitchen chair. "You both seem out of sorts."

"He's not my husband," Michele said harshly.

Elvira's mouth dropped open in disbelief. "What do you mean?"

"We're undercover officers with the DPS. We were pretending to be newlyweds as part of our assignment."

Elvira emptied ice cubes from the tray and fashioned an ice pack out of a dish towel. "I don't believe it! I've never seen two people more in love than you and Nick."

"I'm not in love with him!" Michele stated hotly.

Elvira arched an eyebrow and handed Michele the ice pack. "You're a pretty good actress, then."

"Well, he's not in love with me," Michele insisted, although her pulse rate accelerated at her own words. "What makes you say that?"

"The way Nick looks at you. It's as obvious as the nose on your face he's crazy about you."

"You're imagining things."

"Trust me on this, Michele, I've been in lust enough times to spot the real thing. You guys were meant for each other."

Could it be true? Was Nick really in love with her, and she was just too scared to see it?

No. If she knew anything about Nickerson, she knew he was the type to sweep a girl off her feet. Nick would face love like every other event in his life—head-on. If Nick loved her, he would come out and say so. He'd take charge and declare his feelings unabashedly.

"You're wrong," she told Elvira. "Nick would tell me if he was in love with me."

Elvira shrugged. "Maybe. You want some aspirin?"

She nodded, and Elvira went to the bathroom in search of the pills, leaving Michele alone with her disturbing thoughts.

❧ 19 ❧

Although every instinct he possessed urged Nick to stride into the bunkhouse, take Michele Mallory into his arms and kiss her silly, he knew he could not.

She would misconstrue any such actions on his part as controlling. Nick sat in the patrol car with Charboneau, describing the details of the arrest. It seemed his brain was on automatic pilot. While he talked rationally and calmly about the case to his boss, his thoughts leaped about like a rabbit running from a coyote.

Did Michele love him? Could they ever hope to make a go of their tumultuous relationship? How long could he resist before he told her point-blank how he felt?

Just the idea of going through the rest of his life without her tore a searing sensation across his gut. It would be damned hard, seeing her at headquarters. Running into her in the hallway, smelling her sassy cinnamon scent, watching her stride coolly away from him. Nick clenched his fist.

He must wait. She'd have to come to him. On her terms.

Holding back took an act of pure will on Nick's part and spoke volumes about how much he had changed throughout this assignment. Although perhaps he'd genuinely started to change that night in the truck stop parking lot when he'd realized his hardheaded need to be in charge had almost cost Michele her life.

But what if she never comes around?

That plaintive thought had him shivering in his boots.

"Nickerson, you all right?"

"Fine, Lieutenant. No problem. There's something else I wanted to discuss with you."

"Oh?" Charboneau shot him a glance.

"It's about Michele."

"Go on."

"I couldn't have handled this investigation without her. She's calm under fire, dedicated and hardworking. I'm recommending her for promotion to Trooper Three."

"I thought you two didn't like each other."

"I can't speak for Michele, but personally I respect her immensely."

Charboneau placed a hand on Nick's shoulder. "It goes deeper than that, doesn't it, son? You're in love with her."

Nick swallowed. "Yeah," he said. "I guess I am."

"And she loves you?"

The burning in his gut increased. He met Charboneau's gaze. "She's breaking my heart, Lieutenant. Splitting it right in two."

❧

THREE WEEKS PASSED. MICHELE HADN'T SEEN NICKERSON since that horrible morning they'd driven back from the Triple Fork in total, painful silence.

For three weeks, she'd limped around the station house

like a zombie. She felt as if the very life had been sucked from her veins. Nick had kept his word about recommending her for Trooper Three. She'd just received confirmation of her new position the day before. The promotion was nice, but without Nick, the world was suddenly a darker, sadder place.

It's for the best, she tried to tell herself. Better to end this thing between them before it ever really got started than to dive headfirst into an affair that could only self-destruct.

Forgetting Nick Nickerson did not come easy, and today, the day of Jim Hollis's plea bargain hearing, she'd have to see him again.

Michele entered the Rascal courthouse wearing her patrol officer's uniform. She spied Elvira, Steve Bradshaw, and the other hands from the Triple Fork waiting outside the courtroom, but no sign of Nick.

Maybe he wouldn't come.

That thought brought a mixture of relief and sadness. She wanted to see him again, and yet, she feared the emotions his presence would agitate.

Apparently, his feelings for her did not run as deeply as those she held for him. In her pocket, she carried the wedding band he'd given her for the undercover assignment. During the hubbub following the arrests, she'd forgotten to return it to him.

She nodded to Elvira and the rest, then suddenly caught a glimpse of a familiar figure walking through the corridor toward her. There was no mistaking that regal bearing. Her father, Judge Franklin Mallory. What was he doing here?

She hitched in a deep breath.

"Hello, Michele." He stopped beside her.

"Hello, Father." Her paternal parent looked happier, more relaxed than he had in years. When he reached out to touch Michele's shoulder, she looked into his eyes, and for the first time in her life, saw acceptance reflected there.

"I want to congratulate you on your promotion," he said.

"Do you mean it, Father?"

"Of course I do, child. I love you."

Michele stared at her father, incredulous. She'd heard him utter those words maybe half a dozen times.

"Th-thank you," she stammered. "Your approval means a lot to me."

"Now it's my turn to be surprised." Judge Mallory's smile widened. "I thought it was your goal in life to earn my disapproval."

"Never, Father. I wanted you to think well of me."

"Michele, I've always been proud of you."

"Even when I disagreed with you?"

"Especially then! I like the fact you stand on your own two feet and form your own opinions, even if I don't agree with them."

Stunned by his admission, Michele didn't know what else to say.

"I've got some good news," her father ventured.

"Oh?"

"Your mother and I, well, we've been dating again. We're talking about remarriage. I just bought property here in Marfa. I'm retiring."

"What!"

"Now don't act so surprised. You know your mom and I have a tremendous love for each other."

"But you've been divorced for over five years. What brought all this on?" Michele placed a hand to her temple, unable to believe what she was hearing.

"We met again by accident on a cruise. I guess we both finally realize how much we'd lost by letting foolish pride stand in our way."

"But you and Mother used to fight like lions and tigers."

"And we loved every minute of it, too. A good rousing argument can be very stirring."

"Father!" Michele felt her skin burn red.

"I thought you might like to know. Tell you what, let's grab lunch after this. What do you say?"

"Sure."

He squeezed her shoulder. "I do love you, Michele, more than you can ever know."

"Thank you, Father."

"I'll let you get to your trial."

Could her parents have genuinely worked out their marital difficulties? As a child, had she perhaps misconstrued the passionate, volatile nature of her parents' relationship?

Puzzled, Michele pondered the questions until the bailiff opened the courtroom doors and allowed the spectators inside.

"Katie's transplant is working great," Elvira said to Michele as they passed through the doors together. "We're all hoping Jim gets off with probation and losing his trainer's license. He did it all for his granddaughter, you know."

Michele nodded. She did know. She, too, hoped Jim Hollis would not have to spend time behind bars for his passive role in the racehorse dopings.

She took her seat and tried not to look for Nick, but she couldn't help herself. Her father's words danced in her head like horses on the merry-go-round.

Foolish pride.

Pride and stubbornness and the need to be right were keeping her from telling Nick how she felt about him. Did she want to waste five precious years as her parents had? Did she want to risk missing out on the best thing that had ever happened to her?

But what if Nick didn't love her back?

Now, Michele Mallory, you 're brave and strong. Nothing

ventured, nothing gained. If Nick doesn't return your affections, isn't it better to know than to forever wonder?

Where was Nick? They needed his testimony, and the session was starting.

"All rise," the bailiff announced, and everyone got to their feet as the judge took his place at the bench.

The hearing was halfway completed by the time Nick appeared. Her heart lurched at the sight of him, but he never glanced her way.

I've lost him, she thought in despair. Because of my fears, my pride. The memories of all they'd shared tumbled in on her, taunting her with promises of what might have been.

Even when the judge gave Jim Hollis ten years' probation and took away his trainer's license, Michele couldn't stop thinking about Nick.

All around her everyone was cheering, slapping Jim on the back, and asking eagerly for news of little Katie.

Michele stood up, her palms sweating. How was she going to make herself move across the room? She had to intercept Nick before he could slip away.

And slip away he might. Nick kept casting anxious looks around the room as if he could hardly wait to escape.

Be brave, Michele, do it! She heard her father's voice in her head.

Taking courage from the memory of her father's words, she moved past the crowd, heading toward Nick.

"Nick," she said, surprised to hear her voice squeak.

He stared at her, and Michele thought she might sink through the floor at the impassive expression on his face.

"Yes, Michele?"

"May I speak to you in private?"

He hesitated. Was he going to refuse her?

"All right," Nick conceded at last.

Michele led Nick through the courtroom and into the

unused jurors' room at the back. Her hands trembled; she felt slightly dizzy.

"What's on your mind?" he asked, nonchalantly leaning against the massive oak desk.

"Nick... I..." She stopped, not knowing how to express herself.

"You can tell me anything, babe." He held out a hand to her, and like a drowning victim clinging to a life vest, Michele hung on to his hand.

"Oh, Nick, I've been such a child."

ɢɢ

"How's that?" he asked. It took every ounce of control he possessed to remain passive, letting her take control of the situation. She moved closer, and he put his arms around her.

"You were right the night we arrested Hollis and Felix."

"Oh?" he murmured against her hair. She smelled so wonderful, and it felt so good to be holding her like this.

"I was afraid to love you. I was scared of losing control of my life, of losing myself in our unity. You're so overwhelming, Nick, just like my father. You're so capable and sure of yourself. I felt as if I could never be enough for you."

"Michele." He hooked his finger under her chin and raised her face up to meet his. "Do you have any idea what an amazing woman you are?"

"I was afraid we'd fight constantly. That any relationship we entered into would be doomed."

"And now?"

"I've missed you so much. I can't stop thinking about the 'honeymoon' we shared in that little cottage at the Triple Fork."

"It's been on my mind, too," he confessed.

She curled a fist and rested it on his chest, molding her body against his. "Why didn't you say something?"

"I couldn't take that risk."

"What do you mean?"

"It's the reason I let you go out on Jet that night. You were right about some things, too, Michele. I did keep trying to protect you. But it was only because I loved you, not because I wanted to control you."

The sound of Michele's sharp intake of breath filled the room. "What did you say?"

"I love you, Mish. Probably since the Harbarger bust."

"Oh, Nick," she cried. "I love you, too."

"Can't you see we'd be perfect together? Fighting only spices things up. As long as we don't go to bed mad, we can work anything out."

"We do work well together, don't we?" She slanted a glance up at him.

"You're the best partner I ever had."

"You mean it?"

"I've never met anyone half as exciting."

"I feel the same about you!" She laughed.

"There's going to have to be a lot of compromises, from both of us."

Michele nodded. "You'll have to be a little less messy."

"Okay, I promise to pick up after myself, if you'll stop cleaning constantly."

"Agreed." She rested her head against his shoulder, hearing the comforting sound of his steady heartbeat.

"And I promise not to sing too loud early in the morning if you promise not to keep me up too late."

"Hmm," she growled low in her throat. "That promise might be a little harder to keep."

Nick threw back his head and laughed. "You're everything I've ever wanted, Michele Mallory. A strong woman I can respect. Marry me. Wear my ring for real. Carry my name. Bear my children."

Michele looked into those sparkling dark eyes and felt as if she'd come home after a long, arduous journey.

"Yes, Nick. Yes." She curled her arms around his neck and kissed him until neither one of them was in control.

CHAPTER EPILOGUE

"**A** year ago, who would have thought we'd be here?" Nick stared into the eyes of his new bride.

They were waltzing to "I Melt" by Rascal Flatts. Their first dance as husband and wife. They were in a horse barn converted into a wedding reception hall on the Circle B Ranch in Rascal, Texas. The owners of the Circle B, Sheriff Matt Forrester and his wife, Savannah, had quickly become Nick and Michele's best friends, when Sheriff Forrester had hired Nick as his lead investigator.

After spending time at The Triple Fork and Rascal, Nick and Michele had both come to love life in the Trans-Pecos. And once they'd committed to each other, they'd admitted they were ready to leave Austin for a different kind of lifestyle.

Michele smiled at her man. "A dream come true."

So much had happened since they'd gone undercover together. After the case at the Triple Fork, Michele realized how much she missed horses and decided to leave law enforcement to become a horse trainer.

They'd pooled their money and bought a small ranch

halfway between Marfa and Rascal. Michele would run the place and raise and train Thoroughbreds. They would be near Michele's parents and the wonderful new friends they'd made in Rascal.

"You're the dream," Nick breathed. "I can't imagine anyone else I'd rather go on this journey with."

"Oh," Michele whispered, "we're just getting started. Remember that doctor's appointment I told you about yesterday?"

Nick's eyes lit up. "Michele, are you..."

"Yep," she grinned. "It's time to start thinking of baby names."

"I know one name we're not calling him."

"No Horatio Eugene Jr?"

"No way."

"What if it's a girl?"

"Oh, well then, in that case..." Nick laughed. "Horatio Eugene it is."

"Maybe we'll just call her Jean and leave it at that."

"Maybe it'll be twins," he said. "They do run in my family."

"Wouldn't that be a kick? Two little mini-Nicks running around the house."

"Or two little mini-Micheles."

"Or one of each."

"Either way, they're both bound to be stubborn as hell with us as parents."

"I don't know. I think we learned how to compromise pretty well when we were playing house last year."

"And now we get to do it for real." His eyes misted with heartfelt emotion, and he pulled her closer to him.

Michele glanced around the dance floor at their family and friends. Nick's three single brothers were dancing with three pretty local girls. His mom, who Michele adored, was waltzing with the new man in her life. Her own parents were canoodling in the corner, and their second chance at love filled her with such hope. Lieutenant Ray Charboneau and his wife. Their new friends, Savannah and Matt. The gang from the Triple Fork which included Elvira, who was dancing with Steve Bradford. Jim Hollis, Jenna, and little Katie who was the picture of health and had served as their flower girl.

It was a beautiful day. Michele had never been so happy. Nick dipped his head and kissed her. "I love you more than words can say."

"We're going to have the best life," she whispered.

"With you as my wife, how could we not?" He kissed her again, then dipped her low.

She laughed. What an adventure. There wasn't anyone else on earth she'd rather take it with than Nick.

They danced the night away, both knowing they'd been well and truly blessed by a once-in-a-lifetime love.

DEAR READER, I HOPE YOU HAVE ENJOYED, *NICK*.

If you have the time, I would so appreciate a review. Just a couple of words will do. Thank you so much for leaving a review. You are appreciated!

If you would like to read more Texas Rascals, the next book in the series is *Kurt*.

Available here: https://loriwilde.com/books/kurt/

For an excerpt of *Kurt*, please turn the page.

Much love, Lori Wilde

Visit Lori on the Web @ Lori Wilde

Sign up for news of Lori's latest releases @ Lori's newsletter

EXCERPT OF KURT: TEXAS RASCALS BOOK FOUR

"Oh look, your 'twin' is breaking her engagement."

"What?" Bonnie Bradford rolled back from her desk in the downtown San Antonio office she shared with her coworker, Paige Dutton and peer over at Paige's computer. "Let me see that."

Paige scooted aside so Bonnie could see the TMZ website.

Quickly Bonnie's gaze scanned the salacious headlines: Oscar-Winning Actress Gives Hunky Hubby-To-Be The Heave-ho. There on the screen was Bonnie's doppelganger, young starlet Elizabeth Destiny.

The actress had obviously been ambushed by paparazzi. Her expressive eyes were wide and sad. Her normally luxuriant blond hair, the exact same shade as Bonnie's own, hung in limp strands down her back. Worry lines creased Elizabeth Destiny's forehead and her chic clothes were rumpled.

Sighing sadly, Bonnie settled back in her chair to read the article.

The impending marriage between Hollywood's hottest leading lady Elizabeth Destiny and one of America's most eligible billionaire bachelors, Kurt McNally, has ended quite unlike it began, with a whimper not a bang. The much touted "match made in heaven" has come to a grinding halt before it ever began. Irreconcilable differences were cited as the cause for the split, although there have been plenty of rumors about the couple's real reason for separating. At a press conference held earlier this week , Ms. Destiny announced her intention to seek seclusion during this troubled period in her life. Mr. McNally could not be reached for comment.

The article continued, but feeling slightly sick to her stomach, Bonnie pushed back from Paige's computer.

"I don't believe it," Bonnie said, "Elizabeth and Kurt were so happy together. Anybody could look at their engagement photos and tell that. And I certainly don't believe the two had irreconcilable differences. Doesn't anybody believe in commitment anymore?"

Paige shook her head. "Sometimes I worry about you, Bonnie. You act as if you really *know* these people. I like movies, too, but jeez I don't get carried away."

"In a sense, I *do* know them," Bonnie argued. "I've seen every Elizabeth Destiny movie ever made. I even keep a Pinterest board on her."

"See what I mean?" Paige circled a finger in the air near her temple. "Cuckoo obsession."

"I don't think making a Pinterest boards means I'm obsessed, especially since I resemble Elizabeth so much. I'm just an ardent fan."

"You *are* a dead ringer for the woman," Paige mused, studying the photo of Elizabeth Destiny on her computer, and then casting a sidelong glance at Bonnie. "Maybe she is your long lost twin and you were separated at birth."

Bonnie laughed. "Don't think that hasn't crossed my mind. My mother assures me I was not a twin, but I do feel a certain affinity for Elizabeth. I think she's an incredible actress."

True enough, Bonnie could not deny her lifelong fascination with film. From the time she was a small child, she liked nothing better than escaping from her mundane like at the Cinemaplex near her house. She'd grown up living with her mother and her two spinster aunts and the most exciting moments of her childhood had unfolded at the movies.

She recalled the cozy, safe feelings a darkened theater evoked. She remembered the taste of buttery popcorn, cold sodas, and chocolate-covered peanuts. She recalled the feel of the cushioned seats, the rise and fall of movie sound tracks whisking her away to magical worlds where anything was possible. There was nothing wrong with Netflix, but it couldn't compare to seeing a movie at the theatre. Yes, she was most definitely a movie aficionado and no amount of razzing from her friend could change that.

"I remember when Elizabeth and Kurt got engaged," Bonnie said. "I watched the engagement party on Entertainment Tonight. Kurt McNally is so handsome and he's got a body to die for." She sighed. "A completely masculine male. Every woman's fantasy. And I hear he's a nice guy to boot."

"Ah, you've got the hots for him," Paige teased.

"Yes," Bonnie confessed, chagrined. "I know it's silly but every time I see a picture of him I can't help imagining what it might feel like to have him wrap those big strong arms around me."

"He is one fine hunk of man," Paige agreed, eyeing Kurt's picture on her screen. "But aren't you a little old for puppy dog crushes?"

"I don't have a crush on him. I just appreciate his hotness. I can't imagine what problems he and Elizabeth could have had. They seemed like a storybook couple."

"Just goes to show happy endings aren't what they're cracked up to be." Paige picked up a nail file and buffed her fingernails.

"Cynic."

"I prefer to think of myself as a realist."

"I still believe in love at first sight and happily-ever-after."

"That's because you've never been married."

"True. But I'd love to try it someday." Bonnie sighed again. "If only I could meet Mr. Right."

"How do you expect to meet someone if you never go out? You're way too shy. Instead of running off to the movies, you should be hitting the dating apps. You're never going to have a romance of your own hiding out in a dark theater."

"I know, but I have such a hard time talking to men. I wish I could be like Elizabeth, confident and self-assured."

"Remember," Paige admonished. "She's an actress and probably just as terrified of social situations as you are. She merely acts the part. Next time you meet a guy, try pretending *you are* Elizabeth Destiny."

"I don't know," Bonnie hedged. "Do you really think it would work?"

"You're a beautiful woman, Bradford. I wish I had half your looks. Why do you insist on hiding your figure in frumpy clothes and wearing glasses instead of getting Lasik eye surgery and keeping your hair in a bun? You need to live a little. Hell, why don't you start dressing like Elizabeth Destiny? If you'd let your hair down once in a while, you'd have to beat the men off with a stick."

Bonnie blushed. "I don't *want* to beat men off with a stick. I just want to fall in love, get married and raise a family."

"Then come to the *Fast Lane* with me and Kelly tonight," Paige said, referring to a nightclub she frequented.

"Not tonight." Bonnie wrinkled her nose. She hated drinking and loud clubs and suave insincere men delivering flattery in hopes of luring inebriated females into their beds.

"You'll never change," Paige predicted closing the TMZ website. "Once an introvert, always an introvert I suppose."

Was it silly for her to feel so saddened over a movie star's broken engagement? "It's such a shame about Elizabeth and Kurt. I wish there was something I could do to save their relationship."

"That's your problem, Bonnie. You're too kindhearted. Always worrying about saving the world when you should be taking care of business." Paige glanced at her watch. "Hey, it's five o'clock and I'm outta here. You coming?"

"I've got some letters to finish for Mr. Briggs." Bonnie waved a hand at her keyboard. "You go ahead."

"See you Monday."

"Remember I'm taking two weeks off to do some work around the house," Bonnie reminded her friend. "Gardening, painting, relining my shelves. And I hope to take in a movie or three. There's a new romantic comedy I'm dying to see."

"Oh, yeah. Sounds like a thrill a minute. Have fun living in fantasyland." Paige locked her desk, flung her purse over her shoulder and headed for the door. "Join us at the *Fast Lane* if you change your mind."

Was she really so dull? Bonnie wondered as she watched Paige leave. Did she really dress frumpy? She glanced down at her baggy flower print dress and winced. Okay, so she wasn't a glamour puss. But she loathed attracting attention to herself.

She was a background sort of person, taking satisfaction in doing her job well, a homebody who felt more comfortable as part of a group rather than a leader. She preferred pastels to vibrant colors, easy listening to rap and home cooking over gourmet cuisine.

Unlike her flashy "twin," Elizabeth Destiny, she did not crave the limelight. In fact, she shunned attention. No, Bonnie number one goal in life was to have a husband and children of her own. But would she ever achieve her heart's desire?

"Not if I have to wear skimpy clothes and hang out in bars like Paige," Bonnie mumbled to herself. Whomever fell in love with her would have to love her for who she was, not for some persona she'd perfected. She'd rather be alone than with the wrong person.

By five-thirty Bonnie had finished her work. Everyone else in the office had long since taken off. Extracting her carryall from her bottom desk drawer, she got to her feet.

Too bad about Elizabeth Destiny and her fiancé. If she were Elizabeth, she'd do everything in her power to hold on to *her* man. Especially a man as sexy and masculine as Kurt McNally. Not to mention good-hearted. McNally was involved in a number of charities including building houses for the homeless and organizing fund-raisers for breast cancer research. From what she'd read about him, Kurt McNally seemed the long-haul type of guy who believed in family and commitment.

So what had gone wrong with their engagement?

Maybe Paige was right. Maybe she did care too much about the lives of celebrities.

Still fretting, Bonnie took the elevator to the first floor and left the downtown San Antonio office building where she worked as a legal secretary. Nibbling on her bottom lip, she joined the thinning crowd on the sidewalk.

The wind gusted, twirling dirt and litter into the air. Scaffolding erected to repair damage from recent hailstorms lined the sidewalk outside the Federal Building.

Traveling beneath the plywood-and-wrought-iron skeleton unnerved Bonnie. She hurried through the makeshift tunnel, head down, her high heels clacking an eerie echo against the wooden walkway.

A construction worker whistled at her and Bonnie

blushed. She wished she was bold enough to flip the guy off, but that just wasn't her style.

Maybe Paige was right, maybe she should start acting more like Elizabeth Destiny. At that thought, Bonnie reached up and plucked the barrette from her hair. Shaking her head, she allowed her curls to tumble free around her shoulders.

"Yeah, baby!" the construction worker hooted. "If you got it, flaunt it."

Bonnie scurried along. Okay, it might be degrading to be objectified, and usually she would find it offended, but with the mood she was in, she felt buoyed by the stranger's approval.

She took off her glasses and slipped them into her purse. Maybe she should look into eye surgery, or at the least contacts. After all, she was Elizabeth Destiny's duplicate. What would it be like to live a movie star life?

The wind blew harder. Overhead, a board creaked ominously, but wrapped in her thoughts, Bonnie barely noticed.

She reached the cross street and started to step from beneath the scaffolding.

"Lady, watch out!" the construction worker yelled.

But it was too late.

Squinting, Bonnie looked up and saw a heavy two-by- four hanging precariously from a scaffolding beam by one lone nail.

Oh my gosh! The words formed in her mind but froze on her lips.

"Lady, move it!"

Before Bonnie could leap to safety, a single wind puff sent the board flying free from the chassis to hit her squarely on the top of the head.

ABOUT THE AUTHOR

Lori Wilde is the New York Times, USA Today and Publishers' Weekly bestselling author of 87 works of romantic fiction. She's a three time Romance Writers' of America RITA finalist and has four times been nominated for Romantic Times Readers' Choice Award. She has won numerous other awards as well.

Her books have been translated into 26 languages, with more than four million copies of her books sold worldwide.

Her breakout novel, The First Love Cookie Club, has been optioned for a TV movie.

54469052R00131

Made in the USA
Columbia, SC
31 March 2019